TUPELO HASSMAN's work has appeared in *The Boston Globe*, *Harper's Bazaar*, *Portland Review Literary Journal*, *We Still Like*, and *ZYZZYVA*, and by *100WordStory.org*, *FiveChapters* *.com*, and Invisible City Audio Tours, among others. She is a graduate of Columbia's MFA program.

additional praise for girlchild

"This is Hassman's debut novel, and it's a stunner. Here's hoping she goes on to write more that will equal *girlchild*'s charm and bright, burning fire." —*Richmond Times-Dispatch*

"Rory is like a miniature Margaret Mead, observing and chronicling the life of the trailer park with an insider's knowledge. . . . It's her voice, as well as the offbeat ways in which she presents her coming-of-age story, that make *girlchild* so memorable." —Maureen Corrigan, NPR's *Fresh Air*

"Rory will remind readers of other hard-luck heroines: Linda in Terrence Malick's movie *Days of Heaven,* Olive in *Little Miss Sunshine,* Bo in *Off the Map.* . . . These girls, with everything working against them, clawing them down, rise up, are dignified, tough, and beautiful." —Susan Salter Reynolds, *Los Angeles Review of Books*

"At once a ragtag anthem to the generations of single mothers raising their children on their own, a brilliant critique of the inadequacies of social services, and a colorful depiction of the extraordinary hurdles that children who break the cycle of poverty have to face. . . . Hassman's wildly inventive prose explodes off the page." —Heather O'Neill, author of *Lullabies for Little Criminals*

"This first novel is not like anything you or I have ever read. . . . A testament to joy and beauty, and to the saving power of language wherever it gets a foothold." —Jaimy Gordon, National Book Award–winning author of *Lord of Misrule*

"Rory Dawn Hendrix is a long time quiet before she roars from her mother's trailer in Reno, Nevada. Her voice is funny and pained, confused and outrageous. Tupelo Hassman's *girlchild* is a triumph." —Bonnie Jo Campbell, author of *American Salvage*

girlchild

tupelo hassman

picador / farrar, straus and giroux / new york

GIRLCHILD. Copyright © 2012 by Tupelo Hassman. All rights reserved. Printed in the United States of America. For information, address Picador, 175 Fifth Avenue, New York, N.Y. 10010.

www.picadorusa.com
www.twitter.com/picadorusa • www.facebook.com/picadorusa
picadorbookroom.tumblr.com

Picador® is a U.S. registered trademark and is used by Farrar, Straus and Giroux under license from Pan Books Limited.

For book club information, please visit www.facebook.com/picadorbookclub or e-mail marketing@picadorusa.com.

Illustrations on pages 150 and 222 by Eli Harris

Designed by Abby Kagan

The Library of Congress has cataloged the Farrar, Straus and Giroux edition as follows:

Hassman, Tupelo, 1973–
    Girlchild / Tupelo Hassman. — 1st ed.
      p. cm.
    ISBN 978-0-374-16257-3
    1. Girls—Fiction. 2. Trailer camps—Fiction. 3. Mothers and daughters—Fiction.   I. Title.
    PS3608.A8613G57 2012
    813'.6—dc23

                                              2011041209

Picador ISBN 978-1-250-02406-0

First published in the United States by Farrar, Straus and Giroux

First Picador Edition: February 2013

10 9 8 7 6 5 4

for my cuz

On my honor, I will try:
To do my duty to God and my country,
To help other people at all times,
To obey the Girl Scout Laws.
                    —The Girl Scout Promise

girlchild

teeth

Mama always hid her mouth when she laughed. Even when she spoke too gleefully, mouth stretched too wide by those happy muscles, teeth too visible. I can still recognize someone from my neighborhood by their teeth. Or lack of them. And whenever I do, I call these people family. I know immediately that I can trust them with my dog but not with the car keys and not to remember what time, exactly, they're coming back for their kids. I know if we get into a fight and Johnny shows up we'll agree that there has been "No problem, Officer, we'll keep it down."

I know what they hide when they hide those teeth. By the time Mama was fifteen she had three left that weren't already black or getting there, and jagged. She had a long time to learn how to cover that smile. No matter how she looked otherwise, tall and long-legged, long brown hair, pale skin that held its flush, it was this something vulnerable about the mouth and eyes too that kept men coming back to her. The men would likely say this was due to her willingness to welcome them back, and Mama may have been an easy lay, but I'm cool with that because any easy lay will tell you, making it look easy is a lot of work. Still, no matter how fine she looked, especially after she got herself a set of fine white dentures for her twenty-fifth birthday, Mama never forgot how ugly she felt with those snaggly teeth. In her head, she never stopped being a rotten-mouthed girl.

It's the same with being feebleminded. No matter how smart you might appear to be later with your set of diplomas on their fine white parchment, the mistakes you made before the real lessons sunk in never fade. No matter how high you hang those documents with their official seals and signatures, how shining and polished the frame, your reflection in the glass will never let you forget how stupid you felt when you didn't know any better. You never stop seeing those gaps in your smile.

hope chest

Here are two things of mine: a glass unicorn with golden hooves, the body broken in several pieces, and what looks like a broken necklace. Did I break these? I stroke the horse's thigh, this yes, but the necklace, no. The necklace came to me like this, links of smooth, small pebbles in shades of underwater. Each stone has clasps of metal on its ends or hardened bits of glue from where the clasps, once upon a time, connected. What is missing, what I do not have, is the letter that explains these stones, and what it is I'm to do with them now. The letter was written from my grandma to me on a late Christmas, written on onionskin paper (as she always wrote) and in black felt-tip (as she always wrote) with all of her usual underlines and emphasis, and I remember at least these words . . . *these stones are like the women in our family, some disconnected, some lost, but each part of a greater chain and each beautiful in its own way. There were once many strands, but here are all that remain. It will be up to you to keep them together.* I also know that these words were said better, so much better, by Grandma Shirley Rose. But she's not here. What's here are these stones, this broken horse, stacks of letters in felt-tip and onionskin, a tattered *Girl Scout Handbook*, a welfare file copied from carbon paper, burnt-out votives, shotgun shells, tennis shoes, one green thumb, and me. My name is Rory Dawn Hendrix, feebleminded daughter of a feebleminded daughter, herself the product of feebleminded stock. Welcome to the Calle.

boomtown

Just north of Reno and just south of nowhere is a town full of trailers and the front doors of the dirtiest ones open onto the Calle. When the Calle de las Flores trailer park was first under development on the rum-and-semen-stained outskirts of Reno, all of its streets were going to glow with the green of new money and freshly trimmed hedges and Spanish names that evoked the romance of the Old West. At the first curve off the I-395 a promise was erected of what was to come, bold white letters against a gold background, CALLE DE LAS FLORES—COME HOME TO THE NEW WEST. But soon after the first sewer lines were laid down and the first power lines were run up, the investors backed out because the Biggest Little City in the World was found to be exactly that, too little. With its dry, harsh climate and harsher reputation, Reno could not support suburbs of a middle-class kind, and the new home buyers needed to make the Calle's property values thrive never arrived. Once the big money figured that out, the big money said adios and Calle de las Flores ended before it'd begun.

Broken in half during the first Sierra winter, what remains of the sign still stands at that first curve off the interstate. Warped by the weight of too much snow and disappointment, beat down by too many punches from the fists of Calle boys, the DE LAS FLORES have scattered to the winds. All that's left to speak for the neighborhood that grew up around it is the word CALLE, its two Spanish L's asking why on a desert-bleached sign.

6

roll call

Mama says my brothers were the only reason she'd not followed Grandma to the Calle years before, so when the boys left home to free fish from the ocean with their delinquent dad, we left Santa Cruz and the man who was my father in the rearview. Mama had come to Reno the first time years before that, when she was getting divorced from my brothers' daddy. She'd had to stay here for six weeks to make it legal, and even in that short time was able to find a job, so she knew she could find work here again, running keno or making change, and Grandma Shirley agreed. Grandma used to live in California too but she moved here before I was born, moved for good after living here temporarily to finally escape marriage to Grandpa John, Mama's dad. She found she could escape his memory easier here too. Not only that, the pay was higher and the rents were lower, so Grandma gave up the wet and wild nature of Santa Cruz for the death and dirt of Reno's high desert in order to make a fresh start, and four years later so did we. By then, Grandma had put in her time, marking tickets behind one keno counter after another from Boomtown to the Strip before she eventually got a job tending bar at the Truck Stop right at the end of the Calle. The desert sand of the Calle couldn't be more different from the sandy beaches of Santa Cruz, but the cement and glass and ringing slots of Reno's downtown still felt more like home than anywhere else because this was the first place that ever delivered what both Hendrix women wanted—freedom from their husbands. The Biggest Little City in the World took them in and set them free, and after Mama had paid her own casino dues, she spent months of long nights picking up shifts for the bartenders that came and went at Grandma's side until she finally got called down to the Truck Stop to talk about working a regular shift.

Mama parks next to the Four Humors Ice-Cream Truck, and inside the Truck Stop, the Ice Cream Man himself is parked on a barstool. Mama says that the Ice Cream Man spends a lot of time at her bar but it's the first time I've seen him here, and as we walk past him all I can think about is all that ice cream sitting out in the sun while he sits in here in the dark. Mama sits me at a table by the jukebox and turns my head away from the bar, points me toward the toys she's put on the table. "Stop staring now, R.D.," she says, "and keep your fingers crossed."

My favorite toys are ones Grandma made, crocheted and stuffed: a polar bear with green scarf and hat, a family of mice, the littlest one holding a red lace heart with Grandma's careful "I love Rory D." stitched across its front, a yellow chick inside a cracked egg bright with spring flowers. Every day I bring a different one to show-and-tell, and today Mama had Grandma Mouse and Mama Mouse in the car with her when she picked Baby Mouse and me up from first grade. At first we four just sit facing each other and pretend not to be nervous for Mama over at the bar, but then I start looking through the labels on the front of the jukebox and forget I was nervous at all. There's "Silver Threads and Golden Needles" and "Don't It Make My Brown Eyes Blue" and Mama always has quarters for "Blue Eyes Crying in the Rain" and I like "Me and You and a Dog Named Boo" and I like that I can watch the people at the bar reflected in the jukebox's glass case. There are two regulars I know, the Ice Cream Man and Dennis, but Mama is talking with a dark-haired woman I don't know and can barely see, she is so short and tucked away on the other side of the bar.

I see Dennis has a pile of toilet paper in front of him and I know what he's doing. Every time we come in to say hi to Grandma, Dennis gets up from his place at the very end of the bar, goes into the bathroom, and comes out a minute later. He takes toilet paper back to his seat where he sits squishing and turning and rolling it into the shape of a rose. It's always a rose and it's always for me. The first time he gave me one, he put his empty hand out for me to shake and I felt Mama go stiff and dangerous beside me. Grandma spoke up, soothing, "Jo, Dennis has been here longer than the Truck Stop has." And to me, "R.D., would you look at that flower." I shook Dennis's big hand, which felt too rough to grow a flower out of TP, and said thank you and he went back to his seat. There are ten toilet-paper flowers on the shelf by my bed, and number eleven is interrupted when the Truck Stop door opens and in walks Timmy's mom. I know Timmy from sometimes when we get baby-sat together so I know his mom too, but today the Hardware Man is hanging on his mom's arm and I forget what I'm doing and drop Baby Mouse down the side of the jukebox remembering how the Hardware Man brought Mama in one night after driving her home from the Truck Stop. I watched his shadow over Grandma's shoulder when she leaned down to hug me and whisper goodnight, but he didn't whisper at all when he offered too many times to tuck Mama into bed. He kept offering even after Grandma left until Mama told him loud and clear, "Thanks for the ride, Jack." She said "ride" like a car door slamming, quick and hard enough to break a finger, and that must've been what convinced him it was actually time to go; besides, his name isn't Jack.

I push my cheek against the wall to where I can see Mouse caught against the jukebox in the dark. I kneel down and scrunch up as close as I can, reach my hand through cobwebs and cigarette butts, stretch my fingers, feeling for a leg or whisker, and finally, mouse tail. I hold tight with thumb and finger, and pull. She sticks but she comes out. The heart is unstitched from one paw but Mouse held on to it with the other and I am dusting her off when Mama comes over and says, "Friday *and* Saturday nights, Ror. Come meet my boss."

At the end of the bar, Dennis finishes flower number eleven and messes my hair, and I wish my thank-you smile was loud enough to cover the Hardware Man's voice saying, "Another jailhouse bouquet, Dennis." And to me, "One day a real man'll bring you a real bouquet, hon."

The Hardware Man says "bouquet" like it looks, "bow-ket," and I don't think before I say, "It's *bouquet*, Jack. Like *okay*."

From the corner of my eye I see the Ice Cream Man swivel away on his barstool like he just remembered he's there to drink, but Dennis laughs loud and slaps the bar. I figure that's going to make the apology I'll have to say worth it when the Hardware Man starts laughing too, even though there's not much funny in his voice: "O-kay, bou-quet! Got a smart one here, boys, look out! O-kay! Bou-quet!" He hits his knees and says it over and over, "O-kay! Bou-quet!" until Timmy's mom puts her hand on his arm and says to me, "Why Lori, you've got such a pretty face," without caring if I'm pretty at all. Her bright blond hair is in big silky curls and they bounce when she turns and says to Mama, "This must be the first time I've seen Lori's nose out of a book," and she sure cares how pretty Mama is because her eyes move up and down and get narrow like her voice, but Mama's voice rolls right back at her, growling with *r*'s, "*R*ory is the best reader in three grades."

Timmy's mom's face goes white and dumb and my face goes pink as mouse ears with the hot shame of being smart and rubbing the Hardware Man's nose in it and I'm still burning when up comes Pigeon. Pigeon is the tiny lady with dark hair who gave Mama weekend shifts we can count on, and she cuts right through all the laughter and growling, bends down, and takes my hand. She says my name right, like if she's been saying it all her life, "I expect I'll be seeing a lot more of you, Rory Dawn," and we shake on it, like grown-ups.

anthropologize

The basic subsistence pattern on the Calle is commonly referred to as living paycheck to paycheck. Welfare and disability checks, payroll checks, and the ever rare child-support check are all spent long before they arrive. These checks are supplemented with a collection of surplus or government food, such as peanut butter and certain cheeses. In instances where fresh food is particularly desirable but unattainable, a family eats its way through frozen potpies bought on sale for nineteen cents apiece and waits for better days. Gambling is important to Calle residents, both during and after their shifts at the various downtown casinos, and can be accomplished in several ways, including via lottery tickets, blackjack, and drunk driving. In addition, Calle men hunt and trap everything from birds to stray hubcaps to small girls, using slingshots, shotguns, and the rustle of candy wrappers.

The Calle's economic system is one of generalized reciprocity and enforces the interdependence of the group. Whoever has cigarettes left over after everyone else has smoked theirs is expected to share, with payback assumed on the following first or fifteenth. Whoever is caring for children, their own or another's, is expected to be able to add another child or children to that number at a moment's notice, with little or no talk of compensation. Whoever has gas left in the tank after everyone else is on empty is expected to drive others to the grocery, the cigarette store, the propane fill, or the parole office. This system acts to stabilize the Calle economy and has other important benefits. If the bounty is not shared, for example, the nicotine cravings of one father could cause him to beat his son and the police might be called; if children are left without supervision, even if spotty, or in cases of missing an appointment with a probation officer, the police might also be called. A market exchange system would not succeed here, as all substances, once shared, are considered gifts, and on the Calle it is taboo to calculate the worth of gifts and, indeed, to calculate at all.

The physical punishment of Calle children rarely goes beyond a threat with a closed fist or a slap with an open hand, as both serve to curtail the offending behavior and reinforce the Calle's core values of violence and physical intimidation without requiring a move from the couch. Calle children's role learning is done through imitation of the adults around them; therefore, most will move out at the age of fifteen and begin families of their own. The shame of shared secrets causes many children, especially males, to move off the Calle altogether and not return. In exchange, the Calle receives an abundance of male adults from other neighborhoods who have been similarly separated from their families of origin, and this overpopulation of false grandpas and uncles takes the place of real fathers, brothers, and cousins.

The Government, known interchangeably as the State or the County, is the most feared entity outside the Calle. Its laws are unpredictable and its agents, known commonly as Johnny Law, the Man, or Those Fuckers, are considered difficult to appease. Dealings with the State are usually summed up via the following phrases: "they get you coming and going," "can't win for losing," and "you can't squeeze blood from a stone." Despite the constant fear they engender, official vehicles are rarely seen patrolling the Calle, even to herd up the truant children who blatantly roam its curving streets. As so many Calle teenagers are what the State terms "emancipated minors," a condition most commonly referred to on the

Calle as "grown," and already raising families of their own, the police have stopped bothering to keep track of who should or should not be in school and where their parents are.

The Calle attitude toward sex and marriage is lenient yet constant as necessitated by the fear of being alone with oneself. It follows then that the main rituals of the Calle are first dates and funerals. Because of the effort extended in attempting to make a good impression, a long courtship is difficult to sustain. Buttoning shirts to the top button and forgoing a baseball hat causes emotional upset for most Calle males, and for this reason the wedding ceremony is also kept very short, most commonly based on the following pattern: the couple sits together for a public blessing by an elder in pressed pants and plastic nail tips, and there is an exchange of rings, or the promise of such exchange, and cigarettes. Quickie and drive-through wedding chapels have been erected throughout Reno for just this purpose, turning Nevada into a drive-through state for rites of passage. Both weddings and divorces are handled quickly and forgotten easily, as the many wedding rings rusting through their gold plate at the bottom of the Truckee River attest.

Most other rituals concern the Calle bartenders and involve recovering lost souls who come to the Truck Stop or other local drinking establishments to be revived after their shifts downtown have ended. Bartenders serve the workers as well as listen to the much-repeated stories of those who no longer work, whose dimmed eyes suggest their souls are no longer recoverable, their mouths collecting stubborn white spit in the corners despite how much alcohol is poured into them. Alcohol is often considered the root cause of both the loss and the revival of Calle souls, but in some cases, usually those of young men whose eyes are still relatively bright and whose mouths don't need wiping, it is understood that the bartender, if female and "a fox," may be the one causing the mood swings and not the spirits. Should a patron's mood swing toward the aggressive, he is immediately "cut off," or refused service, by bartenders who are constantly vigilant of a bar's contagious atmosphere. Violence is kept safely at home, as social pressure in the form of being eighty-sixed from any of the local bars is the most important governing factor in Calle society.

jaywalk

Mama makes false starts across the Calle's single strip of busy pavement, the one that separates the Truck Stop from Hobee's. She waits for the delivery trucks and lost tourists to roar past, and when her turn comes she pauses for balance and to check direction. And on some nights that direction doesn't point toward home but right back inside, where the neon flows warmer and the only balance that's worth a good goddamn is the one on her bar tab.

periwinkle

Look at me," Mama says. I've got a color-by-numbers book but I don't read letters yet and Mama is tired of being bothered. I asked her which colors match Four and Seven already, and colored all those spots in, but when I ask about Three, she's had it. She copycats, "Which one's Three? What's Seven? Show me Four." She takes my crayon box and slams the colors out on the table, grabs one before it rolls off the edge, and matches it, letter side up, to the letters that jumble next to the number Four in the coloring book that is filled with smiling dinosaurs and the smiling flowers they eat. The Four I can recognize because numbers are easy and because this one is my own, my "this many" fingers I hold up when strangers lean in and ask, "And how old are you?"

"O-R-A-N-G-E," Mama spells it, her nail creasing into the page as she marks off the letters. "O-R-A-N-G-E. See how they match?" I follow her nail again, this time under the letters on the crayon's label. "Do you get it or not?"

Mama's nail is painted a mean shade of R-E-D like her voice. That's number Two. The red polish she always wears is to cover up number Seven, the Y-E-L-L-O-W her fingers turn from smoking her cigarettes all the way to the end, and all her yelling and slamming makes me B-L-U-E. Number One.

17

I get it.

The flame from her lighter flickers against her glasses, she draws the smoke in, breathes it back out, the smoke comes floating across the table G-R-A-Y, and I pick up the next crayon.

shirley rose

Grandma didn't start out smart, she'd say, and however many years passed she never admitted to feeling much smarter. She didn't feel too smart when she was thirteen and pregnant, and didn't know why or how, and had an abortion on a table in a room in the dimly lit part of San Francisco's Tenderloin. She didn't feel too smart when she was sick for weeks after, crawling from her bed to the toilet to relieve both ends, her mouth lined with fever blisters from the infection that came and went in a flash, just like the baby's father.

Less than two years later, despite the scars and the lessons learned, she had another mouth to feed anyway. My mama. And then more and more, six by the time she was done and finally legal, twenty-one years old. Mama, true to tradition, found herself pregnant at age fifteen. Grandma had been too afraid to tell her daughters how babies happen, superstitious that simply saying the words would bring them to being, and so her daughters found out the same way she had. But Grandma wouldn't put her girls—and girls they were—through the near-death of her own experience, and so Mama gave birth to my brother Winston when she was just three days into being sixteen years old. And then more mouths to feed, and then mine. But by the time I came along, even *Roe v. Wade* had a chance of sticking, and with it, so Grandma believed, the possibility of a Hendrix girl reaching womanhood with more than one choice in front of her. Grandma insisted that I take every opportu-

19

nity, and she never missed a single opportunity to remind me of that expectation. Her superstitions about sharing the facts of life were so long gone by the time I came along that she didn't even knock wood when she told me I'd better keep my legs closed if I wanted to keep my future open.

the great strain of being

From the side of highways all through the Sierras, signs say CHAINS INSTALLED $15. The desperate letters—and if your winter nights are spent on the icy shoulder with semis charging by, you are desperate—are rewritten every winter on the backs of flattened cigarette cartons, on the insides of cereal boxes, and left to flutter, hopeful in headlights on cold nights, on the mountain roads that rush people past the Calle to the casinos that beckon on the well-lit side of these Nevada hills. The signs do their work and drivers pull over, hop out long enough to get the chains from the trunk, while Dennis, sweating inside his Kmart jacket, crawls underneath the car, breathes exhaust, and hooks cold chains together. After an evening on the mountain, he climbs onto a barstool at the Truck Stop and hands Mama bills stiff with road salt, his fingers as bent as his spine, but when his blood flows warm again from alcohol and company and his hands get their feeling back, he gets up to pull a cloud of toilet paper from the roll and sits at the bar shaping gardens of flowers for the lushes and their boyfriends who'll buy him a shot if the timing is right. But on the mountainside no one cares about the magic he can work with his hands. The cold metal sticks to his skin while the people sitting in their warm car above him are impatient for home, where the only thing cold is the ice falling from the dispenser built right into the refrigerator door, ice that is crushed or cubed at the

21

push of a button. The man under their car has gloves but doesn't wear them, wears them only between cars because they slow him down, and he is slowing down enough already. Was a time when he could do eight cars an hour, but those days pass as the younger boys push him farther and farther from the summit.

reno 411

Tahoe's about an hour's drive from Reno and I'm pretty sure our firewood comes from there. Trees that knew the sound of the flowing waters of the Truckee and had critters thriving in their branches now sit in pieces under tarps and carports in Calle driveways to await their fate in Calle stoves. Trees have to be imported our way because, except under the command of Grandma's iron green thumb, nothing grows here. Instead of wildlife all we've got is nightlife. Reno is just like Tahoe, only without anything beautiful, Tahoe but without the fresh air and fir trees, without fathers and sons out for their first fishing trip. Tiptoe up behind Tahoe and put a hand over its mouth. Bear down slowly until it doesn't fight the developers pawing its land. That's Reno. Add gamblers, prostitutes, and tourists so focused on their own thin dimes they can't spare one red cent for each other, then put a blinking sign above it all that says WELCOME TO THE BIGGEST LITTLE SHITTY IN THE WORLD.

dirt

Grandma liked to refer to us as the Queens of the Calle. Here's how she figured: Grandma's trailer was a 1964 Regal, Mama's and mine a 1972 Nobility, and if these homes, despite their lack of sewer pipe or central heating, could be factory-christened with fancy names in curling chrome, then so could we. Despite the lack of even a proper "throne" in Queen Grandma's case, she insisted we have titles befitting the miracle of our design and not the reality of our destination.

To her last days, Grandma could count on having running water but not always on having pipes that made it all the way to a septic tank. Owing to the cost of laying pipe and the trouble of permits, there are usually two varieties of tank in the trailer park: propane and septic. Grandma was always warm enough propane-wise because propane is available in small tanks, get-you-to-the-next-check-sized tanks, but she seldom had such a reliable hookup water-wise, and even when she did, there were risks of flooding, of the system backing up. There's no sugarcoating it. Old septic tanks can't handle shit. All of that glorious bathroom art consisting of grimacing cartoon characters, pants around their ankles, accompanied by witty verse about what can be flushed and what cannot: *No hair combings / use the basket / there's a darn good reason / why we ask it!* These were likely written by relatives of mine and, along with color prints of unicorns, rampant and rainbowed, are the cornerstone of the White Trash Canon.

No septic tank meant that Grandma had to handle her business, her "straightening up" as she liked to call it, another way. Usually the vehicle for this business was a Folgers Coffee can, the big one. And once, when staying over at Grandma's, before she left the Calle, I left something in the coffee can. I was too young to realize that when Grandma had business of this sort she didn't use the can but took herself across the street to the laundry house, and when the morning came and my deed discovered, Grandma was outraged, expecting as she did that I was born with a ready trailer-park instinct, and at the same time, a desire to leave it behind. I learned my lesson hard. The shit we create doesn't ever disappear, especially when we leave it for someone else to clean up.

Grandma did forgive me for the mess I'd left, but not before I saw her crazy rise, bright and blinding as the sun coming up over the mountains on the label of the Folgers can, as she smashed the lid on it that morning, opened the front door of the Regal, and threw the can into the street. Sometimes you can't know what will set a body off, open it up quick and hot and show you in a flash that place inside that's grim as meat and bent as bone, too delicate for touch and too raw for air. Her words went as wild as her eyes, "You're no better than a dog," and left no room for a breath of sorry, so I went outside to get away from the cursing. The can had rolled underneath her old van and I crawled toward it, gravel and grease sticking to my koala-bear PJ's, and pushed until it rolled out the other side. I took it behind the lot to empty it, kicking up desert sand to cover my mistake. Then I pulled the hose away from the house and sprayed the can's inside until it was supermarket shiny and I could see my face in the silver, angry and red. I stomped up the steps and threw the clean coffee can through the doorway onto the carpet, threw the lid in after it, and then slammed the door shut and sat my butt down on the bottom step to await retribution. But none came. Inside there was only quiet.

And then laughter. The laughter went on for so long and sounded so much like my grandma, my usual and safe Grandma, that I couldn't help but laugh too, until the screen door cracked open and Grandma said, "Go wash your feet, girl, and then get inside here and eat some breakfast."

This little lesson in trailer-park etiquette would be the big fight of our lives, but like drunks after a barroom brawl, an understanding was burned between us that would flicker even during a blackout. Sometimes it takes drawing a little blood to really know someone. We knew how hard we could push, but we knew how much we could forgive.

I never stopped bringing my headaches and heartaches to her, in person or in the mail. Even after Grandma got out, as is said in trailer parks and other ghettoes, where leaving is an act of will akin to suicide, in force and determination, and in the loneliness it creates for those left behind as well as those who have moved on. I was as comfortable sharing my thoughts in an envelope as I was at her elbow, and whatever way they found her, she did her lunatic best to solve every problem. Even when it came to the questions I was afraid to bring to Mama, about just what fucking exactly had been done to me and why nobody saw:

16 July 1988, the last hour of Thursday
You're suffering an unhappy time. You need no grand fillip or tired old clichés from Shirley Rose. You've heard them all. So will just write down a hug. Tell you I love you & reassure you that every life is full of "bleep," all well worth slipping in! Everyone "loses" some of their early childhood memories, some more than others. It's a protection device I suppose. When there's a "thing" you don't remember just tell me & we'll "find" it for you.

Always,
Grammers

nobody

The estimated burn time for the average mobile home, top to bottom, aerial antennae to cinder block, drywall to stucco, is sixty seconds, and I do mean flat, aluminum to ash in the space of a "Brought to you by" or "Tonight at eleven." And those sixty seconds are up even faster in homes whose only source of heating are propane tanks and woodstoves, the easiest sources of heat, because nobody needs your social for a gallon of propane and nobody checks your credit for a truckload of wood. Propane and kindling mean it's a safe bet that nobody from the County is going to come down and see how your cables hook up. Nobody checks to see if you're living right if you don't try to do it official.

single file

My family tree leaves men largely out of the picture. I'm making it look like these women bore their children on their own. That's nearly right but that's not why I forget them. The men were mostly bad except for my brothers, who are innocent, and except for my pops, who wasn't bad, just bearded, at least from what I can remember about him, a friendly man rolling onions across the carpet, his beard flashing smiling teeth in my mind. I can't say for sure who left who first, but he didn't come with us when Mama decided we were moving to Reno, where Grandma had laid the best foundation a trailer park family gets by learning the ins and outs of the Calle for us. And whatever I remember, all the men, bad, bearded, or brothers, are long gone, and maybe these aren't my memories after all. Maybe they belong to V. White, "the worker," whose strict accounts of that time before I was born, whose careful renderings of the life Mama used to live, subdue my own muted memories until hers is the loudest and maybe the only reliable voice. And because V. White has such authority, vested in her by none other than the State of California, the golden state of Mama's early, golden years, and because V. White remembers everything with such 12-point precision, I'll leave the judgments and the recollecting and the mystery of my father to her:

girlchild

Mrs. Hendrix has not been at home to receive
several earlier calls from the worker, but she
was at home this a.m., and had company. Some
bearded gentleman had brought her some
vegetables and onions. Mrs. Hendrix's
housekeeping standards continue to be good, and
all her children of school age were in school,
the youngest, Bobby, at home playing on the floor
with the bearded guest.

The purpose of the worker's call was to
encourage Mrs. Hendrix to follow through with
the report from the Department of Employment.
Mrs. Hendrix has taken the aptitude test and the
note from Dr. Crampton, counselor, indicated
that she had not reported for subsequent
counseling. The worker was impressed with her
score, as the test resulted in good potential
for vocational training. The worker took the
liberty of copying verbatim the comments from
the counselor on her results and his opinion of
her potential, in view of her limited formal
education. Telling Mrs. Hendrix of her test
results acted as a real spark, and Mrs. Hendrix
went immediately to the telephone while the
worker was still in the home, and called for an
appointment with Dr. Crowell. She will accept
their recommendations and seems enthusiastic
about undertaking High School completion and job
training, to make her able to provide for

herself and her family independent of her
unstable ex-husband, Gene Hendrix.

Mrs. Hendrix reported that the absent father had
given her $10 over Easter, and again the worker
used this as a basis for the argument that Mrs.
Hendrix would be better off financially as well
as emotionally by getting out of the home and
beginning to do for herself, not depend upon
meager sums from Mr. Hendrix. Mrs. Hendrix will
call the office as soon as she and the Department
of Employment Counselor have formulated a plan.

V. White:wr

4-15-69

We Hendrixes have long been concerned with a number of important things that relate to the Welfare Department, concerned with
these things and this department in the same way a hungry dog is
concerned with the mood of its master and the whereabouts of the
can opener. Some things we look forward to, like food stamps.
Some things we celebrate, like the sweet feel of that envelope on
the first of the month and the ever-loving sound of the postman's
keys on the fifteenth, and some we avoid, some we speak of only in
whispers, like Child Protective Services, an agency whose name
carries such a fearful odor it stays with you longer than the knock-
out stench of a bare mattress soaked through with a child's urine.
V. White was responsible for the bringing forth or stemming of
these ambivalent forces. She kept the record of what my family deserved and what we didn't. This record begins and ends before I
was born, begins a few months, even, before the appearance of the
bearded man bearing onions, who I feel certain is my pops, and

girlchild

soon after Mama's first stint in the town that would later become our home. It begins like this:

CHRONOLOGICAL RECORD

HENDRIX, Johanna Ruth
116 Holway Drive
Santa Cruz, California

Dates of Contact	Office	2-3-69
	Home	2-5-69
	Office	2-6-69

PRESENTING PROBLEM

Mrs. Hendrix, the mother of 4 children, returned from Reno 5 days ago after obtaining a divorce. She was gone for 6 weeks, which was the time required by Nevada law to complete divorce proceedings.

tilt

Grandma couldn't always be trusted to remember anyplace else she might be needed on the days when the slot machines called. She'd say she would be sure to do a thing, be here or there, all of her intentions lining up as sweet as cherries promising a jackpot, but then she'd forget.

If the sun set on a payday without Grandma's van back on the Calle, Mama and I rode to the Silver Dollar or the Monte Carlo or the Primadonna, wherever there were nickel slots making promises even quarter slots couldn't keep. She would take a long last drag on her cigarette before suffocating it in the ashtray and reaching around me to lock the car door, saying, "Do not open up for anyone. Even with a badge." And then she would go in and get Grandma out before her paycheck was going, going, gone.

Paycheck by paycheck Grandma grew to forget more and more, until finally a day came when her forgetting meant more to Mama than any other, when she left me waiting at the school gate and Grandpa Gunthum, in Reno from Sacramento to gamble his pension away for a weekend, took his chance to see me then, the last one he ever took. No matter how much Gun might have changed into an old man bent with regret, Mama's opinion of him never would bend at all, and it wasn't a good one. That Grandma allowed him this near to us was too much for Mama to forgive, so a long silence moved onto the Calle and settled down between Grandma's house and ours, and Mama moved me from Grandma's to the

Hardware Man's house on nights when we needed a sitter. Mama, already deaf in one ear, was temporarily blind with rage on top of it, unable to see that the Hardware Man's house was no place for her child, and there was no one to talk sense to her since she'd stopped talking to Grandma and Grandma had stopped talking right back. Even though I wasn't allowed at Grandma's then, I could still hear them both loud as day, their angry blood pounding, cigarettes stubbing, Grandma's crochet hook slipping.

When they became sudden strangers, Grandma hung up her babysitting shingle, said if she wasn't good enough for her own granddaughter, she wouldn't be watching any of the "Calle strays." The duties of caring not only for me but for all the Calle children under latchkey age landed smack on the curved and sorry shoulders of Carol, the Hardware Man's daughter. Carol, whose shoulders bent forward in permanent defense of breasts that grew too big too fast and forced her to grow up along with them. Her posture didn't change much when the Hardware Man wasn't around but her attitude would, became more like his, greedy and cruel as a casino pit boss: heads I win, tails you lose.

feebleminded daughter

The feebleminded are easy prey. That's what Carol knows as she leads me through the trailer in the dark, shushing my questions and peering from window to window, our trail through the house shadowing the car that has pulled onto my street and is slowing right before my driveway. I'm nearly climbing up her leg I'm so scared, and not big enough really to look over the window ledges without a chair, even if I could get brave enough to let go of Carol and drag one over. For the most part I keep my eyes on her, on the flash her glasses make as they reflect the headlights from the car that is now, she says, parking in front of my house, the car that isn't supposed to be there because Mama is working and Carol, who's been my babysitter for four months already, since I was five and she was thirteen, never has her boyfriend over here, so the person in that car outside can only be a Stranger. A Stranger who can't read because he didn't bother with our NO TRESPASSING signs. But Mama said our signs would bring about as much luck as a twice-used keno ticket in keeping us safe, so maybe this Stranger does know how to read, I think, and Mama was right about the way luck has of running itself out.

Carol and I'd been sitting in front of the television watching *M*A*S*H* when we heard a motor rev outside, and Carol got up so quick out of Mama's chair that its wooden feet thumped and the chair kept rocking even after she turned off the television to hear better, even after she went into the kitchen and looked out the window.

I was right behind her, on my tiptoes, not scared yet but feeling prickly. "Is it Mama?" But I knew I wasn't talking sense because Mama's truck was in the driveway and Mama was down at the Truck Stop, and besides, Mama doesn't have to drive when she's been drinking. There's plenty of men on the Calle keeping their tanks full for her.

Carol shook her head no and reached for the light switch. She took my hand in the dark and we went back into the living room where she slid the chain closed on the front door, me asking all the while, "Then who is it, Carol? Who?" and her saying, "I don't know, Rory, but we should be very quiet. It could be a Bad Man. Let's be quiet and see if he goes away."

A Bad Man and a Stranger don't have regular names because they don't do regular things. There is something about being alone that brings a Stranger and there is something about the dark that brings a Bad Man and there is no arguing with either one of them, so when Carol said "Shhhh," that's what I did.

I know Stop, Drop, and Roll, I know 9-1-1, I know how to call Mama and I know she will come, especially if it's a Stranger because Mama doesn't go for that. But none of these things seem like the exact right thing to do when Carol and I are huddled in the hallway and I'm feeling the possibilities of all the windows and doors of the trailer on my skin, as if they are all wide open and the Stranger outside, in my driveway now, maybe in Mama's flower-bed, is just choosing which door or window he would like to crawl through according to which part of my body he wants to start with.

I don't tell my ideas to Carol because some part of me knows that Carol might be playing. That's what she always says, "I was just playing." And that same part of me knows that when Carol wants to play, it doesn't mean don't be scared Rory, but it does mean don't get any ideas about 9-1-1 and calling Mama, because only stone-cold dummies get ideas like that. So I keep quiet, but I get them anyway. Maybe it's the feebleminded part in me mixing with the crazy part. The part I get from Mama and the part I get from Grandma tangling up inside my head.

Carol lets go of my hand, she tries to, so she can go into the bathroom, but I don't let her. "Ror," she says, "I'm just gonna look out the window, you stay here," but I won't. I won't stay in the hallway alone, in the dark, and I won't let her go in the bathroom either. The bathroom has no way out, the window's too tiny to crawl through, only big enough to see out of, and then only if I stand on the ridge of the bathtub, the metal groove for the shower door cutting into the soles of my feet. And if we're too late and the Stranger's already inside, we'll be trapped in there. At least from the hallway we can crawl quick into my bedroom, or Mama's, hide under beds and in closets, and then out a window. There is never any place to hide in a bathroom.

Carol whips her arm, trying to get me to let go, so I grab onto her with both hands. She is still trying to shake me loose but when I hold tighter she just drags me with her, into the bathroom and over the side of the tub so she can see out the window up by the shower. I start to climb up on the edge of the tub so I can see out too but Carol pulls me back down, my feet landing against the plastic with a boom that makes us both go quiet and hold our breath until she lets hers go in a whisper: "You'll just get scared. You're already crying. Stupid baby."

✱✱✱

Carol hates when I cry. I hate doing it even more, but it's the only thing that makes her stop, and then it only works sometimes, usually at my house, and I think that's just because my face gets splotchy and swollen and stays that way. I'm pretty sure Carol's afraid of what Mama would do if she found out that I'd been crying my head off, and worse, if she found out all the ways Carol likes to make me cry. Carol would be in big trouble and she knows it, and I know it too. Sometimes the only reason I don't tell Mama on Carol is because I'm afraid of what Mama will do to her. It's like I heard the Hardware Man say once when he was telling Carol to be sure I wasn't late for school or she'd catch it: Mama may be feeble in mind but she's loaded for bear in the balls department.

But I'm not, I'm scared as a rabbit, and when Carol steps down onto the tile and says, "Let's hide in the hallway" and "You better stop blubbering or else," I hop right after her and hold back my tears because I'm afraid if I keep it up she'll find her own place to hide and leave me. And that's when I hear Carol make a noise that sounds like choking, almost like a laugh, and I figure that she must be gonna cry too and then I'm really scared. I tighten my grip on her hand and I'm forcing myself to say just one of my big ideas, that we should go hide in Mama's room, pull the phone with us under the bed, but before I can get it out, Carol shushes me.

And the shush she makes has listening in it and fear and the air in the hallway gets slow and distant to make way for the sounds I'm struggling to pull into my head with ears like magnets. And then there's a knock on the door.

All the air in the hallway rushes close together again and pounds against itself like the noise in my ears of my heart pounding because now it's happening and it's at the door and we never called 9-1-1 and we never called Mama and we never found a place to hide. Carol starts for the door, dragging me behind her because I'm too afraid to talk and too afraid to walk, but I'm too afraid to let go too and when I fall on my knees she grabs my wrists with both hands without missing a step and we're over the metal ridge that separates the linoleum in the hallway from the linoleum in the living room and we're past Mama's chair, still now and empty, and we're in front of the door being beat on by a Stranger.

Carol unlocks the deadbolt. I try to get away, scoot backward, tugging my hands away, but Carol's hand tightens around my wrists as she unlocks the second lock and then the chain and pulls the door open.

Through the screen I see the blue workpants with the creases and the tarnished belt buckle and the blue work shirt with the white patch with the blue letters over one pocket and the scratchy black and grey whiskers and the stubby, pitted nose and the metal eyes of the Hardware Man.

"Hi Daddy," Carol says.

"Why are the lights out?" the Hardware Man asks as he comes in, his boots on the rug in front of me where I'm still kneeling, even though Carol let go when she saw it was her own father on the porch and left me to rub the memory of her grip from my wrists.

"We were just playing," Carol says. She grabs my hair, twists it around her fingers. "Get up off the floor, Ror. What are you doing down there?"

recoil

Grandpa John Gunthum rarely came through the Calle and always only in hope of connecting to a family who would have none of him, but his reappearance the last winter he was here cut a path between Mama and Grandma the same as he'd done years before, when Mama was a girl herself. Mama never explained her anger when she left work that night to find that I wasn't being babysat at Grandma's, that I wasn't there and neither was she. Grandma was at the Comstock in the throes of a gambling fit and I was waiting in a pickup on the Calle, the cab lit up so that Mama saw me immediately as she turned her worried headlights toward home, Grandpa saying, "Go on now, child, get," as soon as he saw them.

I was jumping out of the truck even as Mama's tires squealed to a stop behind us, and before Grandpa had barely turned the corner Mama was squeezing my chin. "Look at me," she said, ripping the new doll he'd got me out of my hands, squeezing her too. "Did he do anything to you? Tell me!"

I couldn't keep my eyes off the doll, her dress fluttering, and I said no no no no no no until one of my no's traveled down her arms and into her hands, and she let both of us go. The doll went into the ditch and when I leaned down to get her Mama's voice came out hard and dry, "Rory Dawn Hendrix, I've never been so close to slapping you as I am right now. Leave that doll." And so I left her there in the dirt, left both of them, and ran on home.

babysat

The metal flash of a pair of wire strippers, the unexpected shine on a Phillips head, these things cause the same fear in me, the same gut-tightening, ass-puckering panic as the midnight gleam of a switchblade. Chain locks have the same effect. And lightbulbs. You can find all of these at your local hardware store.

Sometimes Carol goes with Tony to Guido's Pizza and leaves me at Ace. Tony is her boyfriend and he says having a six-year-old around all the time cramps their style, but I don't like him anyway, because when I'm with them he either hogs the Close Encounters game or he hogs Carol and I never get a chance at either one.

Ace smells like orange hand cleaner and WD-40, and I pretend not to hear the adult talk that passes across the counter between the men of the town about certain women of the town as they pay the Hardware Man for their wood screws and drill bits. I also pretend like I never have to go potty. Because I don't need help, but the Hardware Man will want to help me anyway. And when he helps me, the lights go out.

bandages and how to use them

Two girls are separated by a wooden fence from a double-wide trailer. The next lot has a single-wide and a boy climbs the steps of its porch, his leather jacket looks wet in the sun. The girl with long, white-blond hair lies flat on her back and her corduroys have hiked up her legs revealing that her socks don't match. The girl in a gingham dress and loafers crouches in the weeds. The fence vibrates and is still.

"You knocked your wind out."

When I open my eyes the bird's-eye picture rushes away, but what takes its place still feels like a dream. A girl's face is above mine, her smile almost hidden by the kind of curly hair that Mama tries for with the giant metal rollers that just end up giving her a giant headache.

"You fell backwards, right on your back." She crouches over me in the stickers and weeds and waits for me to answer. When I don't, she says, "Ain't you ever done it before?"

I'd just climbed the fence, the *Girl Scout Handbook* tucked into the top of my pants so I could sit and look like I was reading there and not waiting for my neighbor Marc to see me, to maybe say hi to me when he got home, but I couldn't keep my balance when I pulled the book out and now I'm on the wrong side of the fence and my lungs feel like they're the wrong size and Mama is probably wondering where I disappeared to. I don't know if this girl is asking if I ever climbed the fence before or if this is the first time I fell off it or even if it's the first time my lungs and mouth stopped agreeing about breathing, so I just shake my head no.

"Don't worry. You're not broke, just empty," she says. She's wearing a checkered dress with a lacy collar that is gray and stringy and I can see past her big, brown shoes and up her dress where her panties are big like shorts with no elastic at all. I start to blush but she must not know I can see her weird underpants because she stands up and says, "There. You're getting your color back." She puts out her hand.

"I'm Viv," she says, and helps me up. "Viv Buck."

"Rory Dawn." My lungs are working right again. I take a deep breath and stickers poke at me through the back of my shirt. It feels funny and proper to say my last name but I add it because she seems to be waiting for me to, like she did. "Hendrix."

I point over the fence, "That's my house."

"That's a trailer," Viv says, and she laughs. She must be new on the Calle.

I start pulling stickers out of my socks and she reaches down for the *Girl Scout Handbook* where it landed on the wrong side of the fence with us. "Are you a Girl Scout?" she asks me.

I'm so glad we don't have to talk about what's a trailer and what's a house that I tell a great big lie. "Yes."

"Me too!" she says, and holds up her right hand, her palm toward me. Her thumb holds down her pinkie finger. Her three middle fingers point straight up. She stands just like that, waiting, like she did for me to say my last name.

"You must've really knocked yourself out, goose," Viv says after a minute of looking at my face that's turning red again because I know I'm supposed to do something. "Don't you salute around here?"

And then I remember page twelve and raise my right hand, palm forward, pinkie and thumb down, middle fingers extended. I give Viv the Girl Scout Salute and it's the first time I've done it without a mirror.

trail of the trefoil

There's never been any other Girl Scouts on the Calle except me before, and I'm not official or anything. I guess I've never even seen a real live Girl Scout and I didn't expect to, but I've got a copy of the *Girl Scout Handbook*. It wasn't always my own. At first, I borrowed it from the Roscoe Elementary School library, borrowed it over and over again until my name filled up both sides of the card and Mrs. Reddick put it in the ten-cent bin and made sure to let me know that she did. Maybe Mrs. Reddick was a Girl Scout before Dewey hid her away in the stacks and his decimals took over her life. Maybe that's why she put it out for me—she does have excellent posture and the *Handbook* covers posture in detail in Safety and Health under the heading "The Right Use of Your Body."

It's an old copy and it's starting to fall apart, but I hold on to my *Handbook* because nothing else makes promises like that around here, promises with these words burning inside them: *honor*, *duty*, and *try*. *Try* and *duty* I hear all the time, as in "*try* to get some sleep" and "get me some *duty*-free cigs from the Indian store," while *honor*'s reserved solely for the Honorable Joseph A. on *The People's Court*, as in, "Your *Honor*, I was just *try*ing to get my wallet out to pay for the *duty*-free cigs when my gun went off," but these words never ever show their faces together and much less inside a promise.

No one on the Calle gives advice about things that I can find easy in the *Handbook*'s index. Things I'd be too embarrassed to ask, like what are all the points of a horse and how to make introductions without feeling awkward or embarrassed. I can hear all I want about sex, drugs, and rock 'n' roll on the playground, but only the Girl Scouts know the step-by-steps for limbering up a new book without injuring the binding and the how-tos of packing a suitcase to be a more efficient traveler. The only thing harder to come by around here than a suitcase is a brand-new book, but I keep the Girl Scout motto as close to my heart as the promise anyway: Be Prepared.

blocks that little girls
are made of

I'm hanging by a thread, a hair. The fistful that is wrapped around Carol's hand when she opens the door to the Hardware Man and pretends that we are playing a game. That's how come Carol has that grip she has on me. She didn't just twist me around her fingers once, she's in my hair forever.

When I have to stay at Carol's house I stick to the edge of the mattress, wipe my nose with the sheet. Carol says I fall off the top bunk in the middle of the night but I know I don't. I know Carol makes me sleep in her bed to save herself and I don't hate her for it. That would be like hating my ownself. And anyway, it doesn't work. Bad things happen but on the other side of the bed, and I cry soft as nothing and wipe my nose without moving or pulling the sheet or pillow.

At my house it's not all rosy either, but when she sits me at home, some nights Carol lets me stay up past bedtime if I promise not to tell, and I climb from chair to chair peeking through the curtains Grandma ran off on her old Singer, orange and yellow God's Eyes embroidered along the seams. I'm watching for Mama's shadow on the Calle. And when she does come sailing down our driveway,

46

sheets to the wind, I rush off to bed and pretend not to see her through slitted eyelids as she peeks in the door, pretend not to hear her whispered "Goodnight, girlchild. Goodnight."

But I never end up keeping these white secrets from Mama, because their light shines up all my other ones, shows how dirty the ones I keep, the ones I swear I'll keep, really are. It starts with the gray one about not telling Mama that Carol leaves me alone with the Hardware Man so that she can be alone with Tony, and they just get darker from there. I can't keep this little pretty lie for my own, I blurt it out the next morning, "I-stayed-up-past-bedtime," and she's not ever mad because when I say this then she can believe that's it, I've told all there is to tell. Mama needs to believe in my truth-telling. That's her little lie, that it's possible to raise a child clean and safe without rows of secrets somewhere, shelved like the boxes of fuses and circuit breakers at the back of the Hardware Store, coiled like garden hoses forgotten until inventory time. And I need her to believe in this too so she won't start doing an inventory of her own and ask about the places my bathing suit does or doesn't go, the skin that burns pale underneath the Hardware Man's hands.

Carol was brought up by hands used to stripping rolls of wire and wrapping bundles of rope, hands more used to the feel of rubber-handled Vise-Grips and claw-headed hammers than little girl things. She didn't have any time to unlearn that lesson before she was in charge of little bodies too like her own, their skin paling soft between summers and suntan lines. Maybe Carol's memory flips like a light switch too and the things she learned and the things she does fall together in one shadow behind her bathroom door.

✳ ✳ ✳

Carol says, "If you don't close your eyes, I'll cut all of it off," so I do, and the tears leak out because by "it" she means my hair and by "all of it" she means bald. I hear the scissors open and close, the metal scrape of them sliding wide, the grainy sound of them closing slow over strand after strand of my hair, the long blond hair that makes Mama so proud. Then there is a screech of tape being pulled from the roll and the smell of it, plastic and minty as Christmas, as Carol sticks a piece of it to the cut hair and sticks both to my forehead. She slaps my bottom and tells me to "Go look in the mirror. Now." I walk slowly, slow as I can, to the bathroom, my hands still at my sides so I won't touch my head, so I won't feel where my hair isn't anymore, but when I get to the mirror there's only a few strands cut, not a hunk. The hairs hang limp from their piece of Scotch tape but shine gold and white against the red of my skin, and they flash Carol's warning: keep our secrets or everybody gets hurt.

change girl

FAMILY HISTORY   HENDRIX, Johanna #310,788

Mr. and Mrs. Hendrix were wed in 1959. Mrs.
Hendrix was 15 years old at the time and dropped
out of the 9th grade, San Lorenzo Valley High
School, in order to marry Mr. Hendrix who was
13 years her senior.

Mr. Hendrix was a commercial fisherman owning his
own boat. In 1967 this couple purchased an older
but very fine home located in the De Laveaga area
of Santa Cruz. The house payments are in
arrears.

Although Mrs. Hendrix informed the worker that
no one in her family has finished high school or
attended college, she keenly feels her lack of
education. She attended Santa Cruz High School
at night but failed to complete the English,
math, and science courses she was taking because
she went to Nevada to obtain a divorce. She also
took a night course in American Government at
Cabrillo College. She stated to the worker that

she completed this course which is quite an
accomplishment for a 9th-grade dropout.

During the 6 weeks Mrs. Hendrix lived in Reno,
she worked as a change girl in the Nevada Club,
a gambling establishment.

AREAS OF FUNCTIONING

A. Mrs. Hendrix seems to be in good physical
condition. However, she stated that her ex-
husband is suffering from a mental depression
and is in need of medical attention. She states
that he has been having financial reverses
recently, sold his fishing boat, and has begun
applying as a hand on other boats throughout the
Bay. She thinks he is working with heavy
equipment in the meantime but could offer me no
details as to his work or whereabouts.

B. During this home visit, only the youngest
child was present. The 3 older boys were
attending the De Laveaga Elementary School. Mrs.
Hendrix stated that all 3 schoolboys are having
serious problems in school, especially during
the 6 weeks she was in Reno, and they were in
the care of their father. Eugene T., the 2nd
oldest, is enrolled in the special educationally
handicapped class. He is taking 20 milligrams of
Dexedrine on a daily basis. This is for his
hypertension. All 4 boys are supposedly in poor
physical condition, according to Mrs. Hendrix.
However, the youngest boy, who is in preschool,

was viewed by the worker and he appeared to be
in excellent health and spirits. The ages of the
4 boys are:

Winston Dean Hendrix	b.d. 3-8-59	3rd grade
Eugene Thomas Hendrix, Jr.	b.d. 2-6-60	2nd grade
Ronald Joseph Hendrix	b.d. 2-7-61	2nd grade
Robert Dylan Hendrix	b.d. 11-2-64	

C. See earlier paragraphs.

D. Client is uncertain of any support from her
ex-husband. However, up until last week, when
she returned from Reno with the divorce
finalized, he had been supporting the family in
an adequate manner. Mrs. Hendrix is very anxious
to return to Cabrillo and further her studies.
The worker suggested instead that she enter some
type of a vocational training program so that
she can eventually become self-supporting.

EVALUATION AND PLANS

A. While Mrs. Hendrix was able to purchase a
set of dentures before the dissolution of her
marriage, the boys have dental and optical
problems. The boys also have serious school
problems. Mrs. Hendrix is a fine-looking woman
who lives in a well-kept, adequate home.

Although divorced from her husband, this woman
seemed to be on good terms with him right up
until last week. This was evidenced by the fact
that he lived at the home and cared for his
children up until the day she returned from Reno
with the divorce decree.

I have to interrupt V. White before she goes on, and she does
go on, to list Rights and Responsibilities, Eligibilities, Assets, and
Recommendations. I have to interrupt her to say that not everything's as black and white and crisp and certain as it reads on her
carboned copy. Two people can have kind words without sharing
other kindnesses, a man can want to care for his children, can
want to be a father and not want to be a husband, a woman can
love her children but recognize that not all the choices she made at
fifteen are the ones she should have to live by. I have to interrupt
V. White to say that "Mrs. Hendrix is a fine-looking woman"
would seem like a compliment coming from anyone else, but coming from her it is a statement chock-full of suspicion, almost an
accusation.

The Worker was so blinded by Mama's good looks and Bobby's
"good health and spirits" that she couldn't see the truth in Mama's
words. If being fine-looking was all it took, we Hendrixes would've
been the ones to start the Calle and the first to abandon it. Like the
rich folks who first owned this place, we'd take our money and run.
But good looks only get you so far and I'm guessing V. White
wasn't good-looking enough to have to learn this lesson herself.
Instead, V. White's compliment shows what her real questions look
like, the ones they don't print on the forms down at the County
offices but whisper instead in hallways and after meetings:

Q. If Mrs. Hendrix is so hard up, how can she
look so good?

Q. Is Mrs. Hendrix really out of love with the delinquent fisherman, or is she just another lazy piece of trash living on the County?

Q. And is this Mr. Gene Hendrix fine-looking as well?

Q. And since they appear to be on "good terms," what exactly does being on good terms encompass?

Q. Can fine-looking people really succeed in keeping their hands off of each other? And if they can't, should we have to pay for it?

All I know so far is that being fine-looking usually leads to trouble.

trees

In the fairy tales there's only one Big Bad Wolf and the little girl takes only one trip through the Dark Forest and fights only one fight for her life before the story ends in happily and ever after. But life on the Calle is real, not make-believe, and every Calle girl knows that once the My-What-Big-Paws-You-Have fall on her skin, Little Red will carry that scent no matter how hard she scrubs. From that point on, every wolf in every forest of her very real life will recognize her and they'll do their Biggest and Baddest to get into her basket anytime she drops her guard. So be prepared. We're not out of the woods yet.

boom

Here's how the Hardware Man makes the lights go out.

troop

I start my walk to school and Viv is waiting for me at the edge of the driveway. She salutes and says, "Are you ready for the spelling test today?"

I almost drop my books saluting back to her, I'm so excited that we're walking to school together, but I don't remember about a test or even about making a plan to walk to school. Yesterday feels like it happened in pieces, it flashes between recess bells.

"Did Ms. Hyatt say we were having a test?"

"Well, Mrs. Tucker did, so I figure y'all are too." Mrs. Tucker is Viv's teacher. We're in the same grade, but not the same class, and I've never even seen Viv yet at school because our recesses aren't at the same time. By the time my class is coming out to the playground, Viv's is already lined up to come in, so I haven't been able to catch her yet and salute hello.

Tired of waiting for my answer, like always, she goes ahead, "That's okay, R.D., I know them by heart!"

Viv recites our spelling words in a chant as we walk. She chants rules too, "*i* before *e* except after *c*," and doesn't get tired of going over and over them. Her books are all tied together with a belt and she swings them forward with each word, "*i*—before—*e*—except—after—*c*," and "the—principal—is—your—pal."

At the entrance to the school, she says, "Do your best, Rory," and salutes even though we're only feet apart. Then she runs off to the far gate, her books swinging beside her.

the bell

Boys eat bugs in the schoolyard. Newborn caterpillars crawl all over a tree by the kindergarten building. Boys dare each other to eat them whole, fuzzy, green, and wiggling. Girls don't dare or eat.

tip your bartender

The Hardware Man has a counter, not a bar, but he does his share of listening. Men come in to pick up new saw blades and caulking, spackle and sealant, but they get something else at Ace. A daytime medicine like the one they'll get later at Hobee's or the Truck Stop. What the Hardware Man offers isn't that different from what Mama serves up, a friendly face and willing ear and one eye on their money hand.

When the regulars come in, Sonny, the part-time guy, shrinks back from the counter, the Hardware Man moves forward, and the talk begins. Sometimes the order's been called ahead but that doesn't hurry anything and the conversations follow the same direction, starting with the weather. There are only two seasons in the desert so that doesn't take long. Next is work, and work is always a bitch. Which leads right to the last thing, women. And no women are off-limits except for wives, and then only if the husband is in the room. Everyone else is fair game. When the Hardware Man still had his arm around Timmy's mama, I heard all about it, but now that that's over, the customers' eyes fall on me. "Ain't that Jo's daughter?"

The Hardware Man shrugs, like he doesn't know and doesn't care, and says, "Just keeping an eye on her while Carol's off letting her boyfriend feel her up." And the men's replies are always the same. They can't believe that Mama and the Hardware Man don't have something going by now, that she isn't his secret girlfriend. It's the only thing I can imagine feeling dirtier than the truth and I want to tell them she wouldn't touch him with a ten-foot extension ladder, but instead I shrink up against the far wall with Sonny, our backs cushioned by silver rolls of duct tape.

recess

The bell rings the signal for inside dares. Boys sit at their desks and count how many seconds long they can rub their skin raw with the erasers on their Number Two pencils before they bleed. Boys grow up with scars from erasing their skin.

pinball

I'm not very good at it. I can't catch the ball inside the flipper, I just send it faster down the hole, another quarter gone, another trip back up to the bar to measure the number of quarters left in our stack, the number of sips left in Mama's beer. And this is my last quarter no matter how much she's got left, she already said. I'm praying for the ball to cut me a break when a hand puts three quarters along the edge of the glass, and even though I know it's one of Mama's stupid boyfriends giving me more chances at pinball so he can have more chances with her, I turn to say, "Thank you." But it isn't one of Mama's boyfriends, it's Marc, my neighbor, looking almost as surprised as I am when he says, "No, dummy. That means I'm playing next."

Marc is my desk buddy this year. Ms. Hyatt says that even second-grade girls will chitter-chatter if they sit together and our whole classroom, except for Stephanie Harris and Jena-with-one-n, sits at two-person desks in a boy-girl, boy-girl pattern. And she's right. This is already more than Marc's said to me ever. Ms. Hyatt already held Marc back one year, and maybe she thought sitting him next to me would help him do better but Marc can't understand the directions, or doesn't want to, and I hear his stomach growling all morning and he falls asleep at our desk after lunch. He never remembers his homework or to raise his hand before he shouts out the wrong answer, like he always does, and every day my papers come back with smiley faces, plusses, and stars and he gets his name on the blackboard for a million things, like picking his nose and rubbing the boogies under our desk. He has to stay after and pound erasers and his papers come back with checkmarks and SEE ME in big red letters, and every day I'm the only one embarrassed because he's the only boy I like. I try not to like him but it doesn't work, just like it doesn't work when I try too late to catch my last ball before it rolls down between the flippers.

"Too bad," he says. "You better stick to playing Girl Scouts with your new friend."

I look around for Viv, but we're the only kids here and he laughs. "Oh, she's not here, huh?" he says, as he puts his quarter in. "Too bad."

Marc rode past me and Viv on our walk to school together and I made sure he heard us talking about the Girl Scouts by saying extra loud how everyone will want to join our troop. He finally knows something about me, he remembered it, and I almost feel proud, but the way he says "friend," like Viv's a big joke, makes me even more embarrassed than I was before. It's because of her clothes, I know it, because she wears the same dress every single day, but Marc wears the same thing all the time too and I can smell cologne coming off the collar of the leather jacket he's wearing. It's his dad's, and I know he takes it without asking because I've heard his dad hollering from the porch for it, watched him through my kitchen window as he stands at the railing in a T-shirt and curses at Marc when he rides his bike up the driveway and throws it at him. The jacket's sleeves hang so long on Marc that I can't see his fingers as he presses into the machine's buttons, already racking up a bigger score on his first ball than I did in my whole game.

double vision

When we get home, Mama heads for the couch before I've got the door locked, and I'm reaching for the chain when there is a quiet knock that just about gives me a heart attack. I look over at Mama and she is out, her good ear in the pillow and the ear that doesn't work so good turned to the room, so I know she didn't hear. I stand on my tiptoes and peek out the window, scared to burst. At first I don't see anyone, I think it was my imagination, but then I see a head jumping up to see inside and I recognize the curly hair.

It's Viv.

I open the door quiet, and she comes inside like she's been there a million times before. "Viv, you scared me to death," I whisper, and point to the couch and Mama there.

"She's got her shoes still on!" Viv laughs when she sees Mama curled up in her coat with her boots still on but fast asleep. When I shush her she just laughs harder. "I thought your Mama was a mute."

I've never heard anyone use that word before. "She has a bad ear," I say, and I don't want to add that she's drunk so I ask, "What are you doing out?"

"Uncle went out and so I ran over to say hi!" She's so loud, like the loudest thing that's ever been in our house, and I'm worried about her waking Mama, when sure enough, just then Mama rolls over and sits up.

"Freezing in here," she says, before she realizes we're there, and when she finally looks over at us, she blinks. "R.D., what are you doing standing there with that door open?"

Viv says, "Mrs. Hendrix, it's nice to meet you. I'm Viv Buck."

Mama looks from Viv, where she stands in front of our open door, to me, her forehead crinkling enough to let me know that if she wasn't drunk I'd catch it for having a friend over after dark and talking in the doorway. But tonight she just reaches for the end of the couch where her quilt is folded up and says, "It seems like it's time for all little girls to be tucked into their beds, safe and sound. We're not heating up the whole damn Calle." She turns back over onto her good ear and pulls the quilt up. Her coat and boots are still on, and Viv still thinks this is funny, and I'm glad she does, since Mama was just rude in a way I bet Viv's family never is.

Viv smoothes it out, makes it easy like she does everything. "I better run on home then," she whispers this time. "See you tomorrow morning!"

She salutes and I salute back. I lock the door after her, and as I'm pulling off Mama's boots, for the first time ever, I laugh at how silly she looks.

a letter

2 October 1989, 10 o'clock on a Monday a.m.
Morning Pretty Lady!
Bright & sunshiny here in Portola—hope it stays that way—we can sure use
it! Warm up the old bones & maybe keep the old hands working! Many times
when feeling old & tired & "what's the use-ish" I remember & take heart
from your Ma's spirit. She gave much of herself to many. Even her old Ma! Jo
is still with both of us, Child. She gave you your self—by giving you her self.
Strength, determination, courage to do. I know you've got these best parts of
her and a thought strikes me—being her mother & yours once-removed, so to
speak, I remember her earliest years & then her teen yrs. & I remember her
struggle with the whole concept of "Mother." The 2½ years of our initial
(& the most important) bonding was greatly "muddied" by the event of our
being separated & the sudden replacement of me by a "father," at that oh so
dependent age of three. In the space of a few courthouse hours, John Gunthum
took over as both father and mother, almost beating us home from city hall to
get the few of her things he would deign to take. I became history to her & as
time passed I became "his story" of me—almost! At eleven she underwent
another sea change, when by the grace of God and the State of California, I got
her back. Still dependent & insecure about what "mother" meant, in four
years' time she entered the irrevocable state of becoming mother herself. Fifteen
years old, only a few months younger than you are now and one grade behind.
I would & could tell you much of those times, but want to see you settling first
into this age with no one's problems on the table but your own. You need to
figure out where you're going from here first and what of this history is coming

with you. Now it's enough remembering Jo mothering four boys, clumsy at first, Lordy so was I, like a bright five-year-old dusting the furniture. Each time she prayed for a girl—her own little girl! Maybe to give that child what she had missed? From this advantage of time, it seems likely. You, Ror, were her dream & you fulfilled it—you are still doing it—you always will! Know it, Child & be glad & proud (a little!) & happy! When it is time for you to hold your own child you will automatically—

and interruptions

It always seems Grandma is fooling in this letter, one-too-many gin beers leading her to trite talk about the dead, about the type of mother Mama might have been if she'd become a mother on purpose, maybe, or gotten a later start at it, or liked living well enough in the first place that introducing the option to a little face not unlike her own would be a fine idea. Grandma's thinking is that when and if my time to be a mother ever comes, I will step into the role that terrifies me more than any and with some confidence that I know what it means. Mother. That's what all Grandma's underlines and exclamation points are for, to try to make me believe a thing I know she lost faith in a long time ago, as if extra ink can make up for using the wrong words in the first place, can turn a lie into the truth or blot out all the mistakes a Hendrix ever made in caring for her children and letting them go. Grandma couldn't hold on to Mama and her sisters, Grandpa's pathologies hid so much more obediently than did hers, hiding and biding their time. The State awarded Grandpa all four of his daughters, in gingham dresses and throats collared with lace, and he grabbed on to them with both hands, tore them apart, and put them back together so confused that by the time Grandma had pushed the custody papers through every in- and out-box of the State of California to get them back, her girls thought she was the enemy. Their mother's return shined a light on their pain, and like little girls always do, they thought this meant she was the one to be feared while the man with the big hands, who had used them in ways they would spend their lives struggling to overcome, was thought of with longing as dirty and chewed as his fingernails.

Grandma couldn't save them so she's trying to save me. Mama couldn't do it. She might have thought she was ready after raising four boys, but the reality of having her own little girl and all I reminded her of deafened her to the real dangers that surrounded us, so Grandma tries to make up for that, but too late and at too great a distance. Mothering is not this family's strong suit. The missing places at the table prove it. Mama's got four sisters she wouldn't talk to, a brother she wouldn't talk about, and I've got four grown brothers of my own who show up here only when driven by crisis or guilt, their eyes red from staring down the lines of the highway. My brothers are like all the men in Mama's life, mostly memory to her, blurred as the postmarks on the random Christmas and Mother's Day cards sent from Sacramento and Frisco and any city that held them far away and safe from what happened to them under Mama's roof. I know the stories about Grandma's failures in the mothering department, and when it comes to Mama I could tell plenty of my own, but my brothers' story tops them all.

Still, as much as I have thought about this, used these failures to dismiss the very idea of bringing any more Hendrixes into this world, Grandma succeeds in reminding me of one thing, a small thing that lets me know that she is telling a truth in there somewhere. That there is a tenderness that runs quiet but sure in our blood and reveals itself as dependable as bedtime. It is the memory of Mama tucking me in at night, a name she had for me in the darkness. In the mornings when she woke me for school, I was always *Sunshine*, but at night I was always always *girlchild*.

I could include a letter here from Mama to prove it. I've got stacks of them, ones she wrote me on late nights by cigarette light, after the words we tried to use out loud gave out. Torn apologies on the backs of envelopes, her hand as shaky as her spelling, stubbornly stacking up words to put out the fire of the night before. They were letter writers, correspondents, these women, besides being high school dropouts, unwed mothers, welfare moms, alcoholics, gamblers, smokers, ragers. When Grandma finally moved off the Calle, in part to escape these definitions, obvious as stained sheets on a line, her letters to me started to arrive. But no matter when or where they put pen to paper, Mama's and Grandma's handwriting echo each other. I see the same strokes in my own hand, the same tilt, but unlike Grandma Shirley's proper capital *I*'s, Mama's are all lowercase, and unlike both of theirs, mine are long, slashes on the page. And while Grandma called me *"Dearest R.D."* and *"Sweet Ror"* and *"Rory Dawn Rising Bright,"* Mama's letters to me bore no greeting, but began with just that word, her word, *girlchild.*

The letters are sitting right here, bound in dirty string so they can't come open too easily, so they can't steal my nights as I look for secrets in their creases. Mama developed Grandma's preference for onionskin paper too, and felt-tip, I wait for this to happen to me, I'm certain it will. The only way to tell the difference between Mama's letters and Grandma's at first glance is that Mama's stay bundled up so tight the string rips into their pages and Grandma's are loose and open, all over this table. I keep Mama's letters closed, keep their edges close together like a cut that needs force to heal. I'm all wrapped up in there, jumbled with her, small *i*'s and slashes, her story in my story at every turn.

"Look at me," Mama says, it's early morning and her eyes are clear, on level with mine, but all I feel is the tightness of her hands around my wrists and the pull of the skin on my forehead. We've just finished fixing my hair. She brushed it back into two tight ponytails with pink yarn in bows, and my tummy hurts from the cussing and pulling and yelling to "sit still" and "do you want to do this or not." Mama is no good at fixing hair but today is picture day and pictures mean I get my hair yanked and pictures mean I have a dress on and dresses mean we have the talk.

She shakes my wrists. "What is the rule?"

I want to cry from the stupid words I have to say and the pull of the stupid rubber bands on my hair and how stupid she is for not knowing how to make a stupid ponytail without stinking up Christmas with cusswords and cigarette smoke, but instead I say it, I make myself say it, "Never let anyone touch me where my bathing suit goes."

One of my arms is released as Mama reaches for her cigarette. "I'll kill anyone," she says, through her fingers as she brings it to her mouth, "who tries," and I believe her, because of the way her eyes squint as she takes a drag, take the measure of a thing I have never been able to see but that she can never seem to get away from. That dark thing that loves bare legs and bathing suits and makes us say these words to each other to fight it off. The words don't work, they haven't worked yet, but Mama seems to think they do, seems to think they will, so I keep saying them even though they make my skin prickle up, I say them, and I feel air coming at me as if I didn't have a dress on at all, as if I was actually standing there in my bathing suit, skin cold from the water dripping off of it.

It's all triangles, top and bottom. Two triangles meet on my chest and make me nervous. They slip easy and I don't notice sometimes because I'm underwater and underwater I can move fast or slow and I can have the longest legs but no one can see me and say, "Look at those long legs," or talk about when I get older and how far up my legs will go. Underwater they are just my legs and my bathing suit can go all around and in and out and it doesn't matter. The Hardware Man doesn't matter. When he comes to the lake I

71

run to the water and take cover and even as he's backing his boat up onto the sand I float on the waves he makes and even when he's parking his truck and taking Carol out for their first run I lie back, safe, in the warm trail left by his exhaust. Mama watches from the shore and I know that she is busy with sandy cans of Coors and trying not to worry about the water, trying to remember that she wants me to do things she never could. As the gas and oil mix with the water of the lake I feel her worries brush across me, leave a trail of chicken skin.

Mama never learned how to swim. She can't hear out of one ear and gets turned around underwater. She'll kick all the way to the bottom, thinking she's on top. She won't even sit in an inner tube, even if I tie it to a tree and the water only comes up to my tummy, even if I hold her cigarettes and beer so she can get in. And she won't set foot on a boat, anyone's boat. I'm allowed though because she says one difference between her and me will be, when my time comes, I won't have any fucking idea how to drown.

Grandpa had a gun and it ruined Mama's hearing. He was an angry man and he liked to celebrate it. He liked best to have Mama and her sisters dress up, line them all up, and make them stand close while he'd fire his shotgun off, the blast cracking through the air above their heads as sure and painful as if he'd emptied the barrel right into their bones. She still has dreams about it, gingham and butterfly-collar nightmares that scream through the house. She dreams about it sometimes when she's awake too. She talks to the thing I can't see, mistakes the Christmas tree for it, or the coat rack, and tears it down. I can't get in there with her where she's fighting, kicking out at whatever's pulling her away. I wait for her to come up for air, I put her to bed, put the Christmas tree back up, pick up the coats, double-lock all the doors, and tuck myself in.

wings

What's your house like?" I ask
Viv, and push my arms and legs to make deeper marks in the field
where we are lying together and making dirt angels.

Viv already said she's not allowed any company and told me,
"You wouldn't like it, Rory Dawn, because Uncle gets meaner the
longer the days goes on. He says I'm so stupid the only scout troop
I could ever belong to is one that troops off a cliff, says I'm feebleminded like all the women in our family, like all the women in the
world!"

I'd tried to imagine anyone calling Viv stupid. "I got an uncle
like that," I'd said, and she'd nodded.

She said she knew that I did, and when I asked her how, because I never talked about the Hardware Man, she'd said, "I could
just tell, that's probably why we're in the same troop!"

Ms. Hyatt has just taught us about exclamation marks and how
they do the same work as a period but in a bigger way, to show
emotion. Every time Viv talks, I feel an exclamation mark, POP!,
in my head, like her sentences all end this way. It's a way that
makes me feel like we're really true friends, best friends, like Stephanie and Jena-with-one-n who get to sit together, and how if we
were in the same class we'd sit together and write BEST FRIENDS
4-EVER with a hundred exclamation points like the ones Viv uses
to answer my question now.

"My house is like yours but sunk in the ground so it can't go

73

anyplace. Not like your . . ." she pauses before she says it, she's still getting used to not calling it a trailer, "house!" She swings her arms and legs fast, pushing like me but harder. "Your house could go places!"

"Nope," I say, finishing my wings and getting up, careful not to mess my angel's skirt. I help Viv up, and we brush twigs off each other and check our work, two angels flattening the sage. "It just looks that way."

stucco

Single-wide, double-wide, a house with a hitch. Single mom, gravel drive. Propane by the gallon, generic cigs by the carton, and solitaire round the clock. Cousins and animals multiply like cars in the front yard. Nothing around here gets fixed.

The Calle is not a through street. The road is paved with uncles. Smokey, Barney, Johnny Law, Pig, uncles with their badges, with their belt buckles, say, "Hey Sugar, Toots, Sweet Thing, is your mama home?" hand already through the already ripped screen door, finger on the latch.

"When you play solitaire you're playing against the Devil," the Calle Grandmas say through false teeth, yella teeth, broken teeth, through pink gums hidden behind hands paused from stringing garlands of silver beer tabs. Hands that threaten to shuffle the spots off the cards, threaten to "smack you so hard your no-good daddy'll fall outta bed" if you don't stop interrupting the idiot box with your idiot mouth and see to that mess in the kitchen.

Fifty-two pick-up. Suicide kings and one-eyed jacks face off on orange shag. Calle girls cry uncle through clenched teeth and past his shoulder the sirens flash redneck blues across the white-stucco, nicotine-yellow ceiling.

boom

Here's how the Hardware Man makes the lights go out. I say I have to potty and he says that he will help me, and takes my hand, and we go to the back of the store through aisles of fan blades and boxes of electrical tape to the bathroom that is supposed to be for girls and boys, but I think really only for boys, because there are boot prints all over the tile and the soap is dirty. I can't reach to turn on the light. The light is at the top of the ceiling and turns on with a chain that you pull once for on and twice for off, but it's high above the sink and I can't reach it even if I stand on the seat.

The Hardware Man can reach it, though, and he pulls the chain once and closes the door. And he locks the door and undoes my pants, he says because I am little and I need help going to the bathroom. He always says that, just like he always says that good little girls like me should wear dresses. But I always wear pants. Mama doesn't like dresses and he knows that but he also knows that I can go to the bathroom by myself so I don't tell him anything. And then I forget all about having to pee because he is telling me to lie down on the floor and I think how the boot prints are going to get all over the back of my new favorite shirt with the rainbow on it but then he is telling me to be good, which means not to make noise, and I stare up at the lightbulb and the chain that is still swinging until the patch on his pocket that says Ace Hardware blocks it and then it doesn't matter if he pulled the chain once or twice or how much noise I make because everything is dark and quiet, except for the word *good*. *Good* is in my ears over and over again, and sometimes it is cut up in pieces of a whisper and sometimes it has more *o*'s than it needs, and always it is so heavy I can't breathe and my shirt is all ruined.

the electric company

Does that feel good?" Carol asks me, and her friend Trina laughs and coughs on the smoke that comes exploding out of her mouth. "Does it?"

Carol and Trina were listening to Meat Loaf and getting stoned, and I was sitting on the top bunk where I'm really not allowed to be until I'm "ten, if I'm lucky," trying not to make any noise so Carol won't tell me Get Down from There and that's when Carol got up from the radio and said, "Let me show you something." She was talking to Trina but coming over to me. "Come here, Ror."

She took my book and I watched it go, my page gone, and then she lifted me onto her hip. "Okay, watch," she said, putting her hands on my bottom and moving me in circles against the hip pocket of her corduroys, against her hip, against her hip bone.

I pretend like I can't hear her asking. I keep my eyes on the top bunk, on the cover of my book, it has green cloth and gold letters, I read the words over and over to keep my eyes off the curly red bangs and the smoky cloud that hang around Trina's laughing head, *Girl Scout Handbook*, it says, *Girl Scout Handbook*, and the outline of the trefoil behind it, the points of the promise.

"Come on, Ror," says Carol, "doesn't that feel good?"

"G-O-O-D," I say, and grip the arms of my chair. The man, who is sitting at Mr. Lombroso's desk even though he is not the principal of Roscoe Elementary School, smiles and makes a note with his brand-new pencil.

"Gear," he says.

I swing my legs.

"G-E-A-R," I say back to him, and swing my legs higher so they come out straight, so I can see them. I'm wearing a skirt today. It has gray flowers and three ruffles and lace. I hate this man who treats me like I'm a great big insect in his very own mason jar. I like my new skirt.

"Theme."

"T-H-E-M-E." I have to dress up for this man with the new pencils and briefcase whose leather is almost as shiny as the gold locks he flipped open at once, SMACK!, when Mr. Lombroso brought me in. I have to dress up for his briefcase.

"You're doing very well." He smiles at me. "Queen."

I spell to the wall behind his head. I swing my legs after every letter, "Q-swing-U-swing-E-swing-E-swing-N-swing." I will for his pencil to break, for one of my tennies to fly off and hit his round wire glasses.

"Wash," he says but I can't hear him right.

"Wash or watch?"

He is delighted. "Can you spell both?"

Carol is babysitting Timmy and me together. Carol is Timmy's aunt. Like the same way the Hardware Man is my uncle. Not in real life.

It is Timmy's bath time and Carol turns on the water in the tub. She calls me into the bathroom.

"Get undressed, Ror," she says, as she pulls down Timmy's pants. Timmy is barely five years old and I am almost eight. Timmy's still stuck on the kindergartener's side of the playground. Timmy is holding a Lego and licking it.

"But I already took a bath," I say.

"Get undressed." She coos at Timmy as she moves the Lego out of his mouth so she can pull off his shirt.

"Carol, I took a bath." I did. I just took a bath.

"Took a bath!" Timmy yells. "Took a bath!"

"Do it," she says and there is metal in her voice. I start to cry. I unbutton my pants slowly, quiet, like the way I'm crying, my mouth wide and silent, spit stringing. I push my pants down. I put my thumbs on my panties but I can't push them, all my strength is in my stretched mouth, my tight-closed eyes. But Carol is sitting on the toilet seat so she can keep an eye on Timmy, who is splashing in the bathtub, and me at the same time, and she yells into the hallway, "Now. Rory."

In the bathtub I can't have any toys and she won't let me play with Timmy's because she says I am too big for that. She won't let me have a washrag because, she says in a copy-catter voice, "You already took a bath so you must be clean." I'm not allowed to do anything but sit cross-legged next to Timmy, who is used to me crying, and motorboats his Lego through the water and laughs. Carol sits on the toilet seat and stares at me until the water finally grows cold enough to make Timmy start to fuss and then she lifts him out of the tub. She starts to dry Timmy off and as she wraps him in the towel and takes him out of the bathroom she says, "Get in bed."

The lights are always going out now. It happens when I'm with Carol a lot, but never at school and never with Viv. Mama is working nights at the Truck Stop, and when she's not working there she's working graveyard at the Primadonna so I'm almost always with Carol. I must be saving all my electricity to use during school-time, I think, and that's why Mr. Lombroso learned my name and why people with briefcases started showing up in his office to ask me the same questions over and over and why I got a new skirt and why Mama, when I do see her, started looking at me like I'm going to lay an egg.

outlier

Wait," the Briefcase Man says.

"Verb or noun?" I say, and swing my legs and wish for a harder question. I want a question that takes all the electricity I've got and blows me into a million pieces.

"Wait," the Hardware Man says. He tells Sonny to watch the counter at the Hardware Store because he's going to take me for burgers. Sonny's always talking about how he's ready to man the counter himself but he never looks happy when the Hardware Man says he's taking me to pick up lunch. He stands at the door with his arms crossed, watches us get into the truck and drive three stores down to Pete's Liquor where the Hardware Man leaves the engine running and goes inside.

I do not swing my legs in the Hardware Man's truck. The floor is covered with empty cups and beer bottles and hamburger wrappers and junk and the seat is covered with cloth that is stiff from being spilled on. It's hard where it should be soft and I try not to touch it. I don't want to touch anything, but still, when I see the Hardware Man through the window with his back to me, I reach down

82

to the trash under my feet and turn over a piece of glossy paper. A lady's face stares up from between my fingers. Her flat face is all *O's*. *O's* around her blue eyes and on her pink cheeks, and the red that makes her two lips is a big empty *O*. Her picture is in a bad kind of magazine, not for play and not for kids. I know what it is now, but I'll forget again as soon as it gets dark.

When I told Mama I wanted to get rid of my dolls and only have books, she was thrilled. When I started keeping them in ABC order, she called Grandma to tell her even though she hadn't dialed Grandma's number in so long I thought she'd forgot it. I wanted her to do something that had less to do with pride and making telephone calls and more with worry from seeing that all these letters can't be lining up to spell anything good, that I should be getting invited to sleepovers instead of getting perfect grades, but that was all she did. Act proud. Like all there is to getting by in life is knowing your ABC's.

"Enough."

That's what Carol says and she says it mean. Even though I'm always way over on the edge of the bed and not making noise and breathing through my mouth and letting the snot run onto the sheet so I don't sniffle, she says it.

"E-N-O-U-G-H," I spell to the Briefcase Man.

I am pushing against the wall because I don't want to touch her and I don't want to feel the Hardware Man touching her and I

83

don't want his big dirty hands pulling my hair. Carol says, "Wait," even though the bed is already sunk from his weight and I'm squeezing into the crack that is growing between the mattress and the wall, growing bigger and bigger with each push he gives on top of her, she still says it. She even says, "No," somehow, and sometimes it has an echo at the end of it, the *o*'s rolling back. And sometimes the echo goes on so long I think that she is the one crying and I am the one getting pushed, pushed silent, like a *k*.

"No."

"K-N-O-W."

flicker

Here's ▮ the Hardware
Man's house ▮▮▮▮▮▮▮▮▮▮
▮▮▮▮▮▮▮▮▮▮
▮▮▮▮▮▮▮▮▮▮
▮▮▮▮▮▮▮▮▮▮
▮▮▮▮▮▮▮ my mouth
all the time ▮▮▮▮▮
▮▮▮▮▮▮▮▮▮▮
▮▮▮▮▮▮▮▮▮▮
▮▮▮▮▮▮▮▮▮▮
▮▮▮▮▮▮▮▮▮▮
▮▮▮▮▮▮▮▮▮▮ don't fuck-
ing say anything ▮▮▮ don't fucking say anything to anyone
ever.

opening my fist is telling

i hate Rory D.

slants   slashes

uncle

The metal smell of Ace in the mornings makes you sick, leaves you coughing up last night's gin and tonics on the bathroom floor while the grease spots on the tiles turn the colors of a little girl's rainbow T-shirt. You become a dervish with mop and bleach to erase the colors from the floor, but then the smell of bleach is too like your own smell and you are sick again, crouching, trying not to ruin the knees of another dark uniform with circles of bleach that remind you of what you should have already learned by heart, having taught the lesson so well: There's never anyplace to hide in a bathroom.

You've done a thing you can't clean up, found a place you can't reach with mop or apology. The forever you've created branches like the hairline fracture in a pelvic bone, hides like a dirty Polaroid shoved under a mattress, rises like hot blood to burn cheeks pretty with shame. Places you didn't even know you were signing your name will always be marked with your hand, but despite every new day's resolution to never do it again, you will. You'll look away from your own face in the mirror, pull the chain twice to hide from yourself in the dark, and when it's all over you won't fucking say anything. You won't fucking say anything to anyone ever.

ma bell

Mama and Grandma must've made up the day she called to tell her about my book rearranging because our schedule got rearranged right after that, and now I'm allowed to stay at Grandma's again after school and when Mama's working nights. And they must have agreed with the Briefcase Men that I'm getting pretty smart too, because today Grandma said I could go to the playground if I stop by the Truck Stop before and after and check in with Mama. She calls Mama to tell her so, they sound easy on the phone, and before they hang up, Grandma says, "We'll get her back yet." I guess they're worried I won't come home but I'm going to follow the directions perfectly so I'll get to go again.

On the way to the Truck Stop, I'm passing the Hardware Man's house and I just slow to look in his windows when someone pokes at my shoulder. I shouldn't have lagged, I think, now I'll never get to go to the playground by myself again and I love the playground when school's out, when it's no one but me and the swings.

But when I turn, it isn't the Hardware Man's face, or Carol's, like I expected. It's Viv. She pulls my arm. "Come on, R.D.," she says, "let's go swing!"

"Viv!" I haven't seen her for days since the Bucks don't have a phone so I couldn't call and tell her about staying at Grandma's. I've been walking to school by myself again and I'm so excited to see her that I'm using her exclamation points without even realizing it,

POP!, "I have to stop into the Truck Stop first. You can say hi to my mama!" Viv has been pulling my hand, making us run, but when I say this she slows.

"I'm not supposed to see nobody." Viv doesn't say things wrong like Calle folks, she's good about double negatives, so I know this means she really doesn't want to go.

She says, "I'm not supposed to go into drinking establishments." That's the way she talks, formal, like a book from a long time ago, and I think her family must all talk like this, like her house is still in black and white with dinner on the table and no phone ringing.

"The Truck Stop is a bar," I tease her, "but you can wait outside while I run in. Okay?"

This works. "Okay, but be quick so I don't catch it," she says, and we run on.

At the Truck Stop I'm barely in the door before Mama's on the phone with Grandma and giving me the thumbs-up for coming straight down. I climb up on a barstool and give her a kiss and hop right down like I'm supposed to, but when I see her start making me my usual, a Shirley Temple with more than the legal limit of maraschino cherries, I say, "I'm not thirsty, Mama. Besides, Viv is going to the playground too, she's waiting outside."

Mama is surprised. She stands there frozen, the jar of cherries in her hand.

"You remember Viv, we walk to school together." I turn to the door and shout over the music from the jukebox, "Wave, Viv!"

I see the flutter of her dress as she steps in the doorway and waves quick, "She's not allowed inside 'cause—" and just then I learn that what Grandma says about Dennis is right, he's the true gentleman of the Calle.

"A friend of R.D.'s doesn't only deserve a wave, she deserves a bow," he says, and he does it, leans down from his barstool and bows at Viv's shadow in the screen door. I hear her giggle. "And a flower." Dennis hands me two toilet-paper flowers this time, one for me and one for Viv, and Mama seems to relax.

"Remember the rule, one hour and stop by here on your way back so I can call Grandma," she says; her hand is already on the phone to call Grandma again as I wave my flowers and run out the door.

Viv is careful with her flower all the time she's swinging, she says it's the most beautiful thing she's ever gotten, but when our hour's up she asks if I'll keep it at my house since her uncle will want to know where she got it. I do, of course. I have a garden of Dennis's flowers on the shelf by my bed, and when I get home I put Viv's right in the middle.

okay bouquet

I pluck Dennis's flowers from the shelf, one by one. I hold them when I sleep to keep my mouth shut tight, but in the morning my mouth is red from the Truck Stop's cheap toilet paper, which is good at folding into the shape of a rose but hard on soft skin. I pick another flower to hide the red and carry it all day.

shoot

I've been keeping my mouth shut but this morning the silence isn't my fault. There's no school today and no Grandma's either because snow snuck down quiet and deep last night, buried the roads and our front porch and there's no driving until they're cleared. No matter what, I haven't told Mama anything because the Hardware Man said not to, and even though he's gone I know he meant it. And I'm not telling her now because I don't want to start an avalanche, don't want to shake all that we've built up out from under us, send us sliding back to where we started. If she thinks everything's all right, everything is all right, and so I keep the words in but they curl tight in my throat and under my tongue and sprout out of my lips like bean sprouts twisting up from the egg cartons on Grandma's windowsill. I keep holding my hands over my mouth, watch TV over my fingers, go to bed with both hands under my nose in case one falls away and the truth comes pouring out in my sleep, but I must have Grandma's green thumb too because red blossoms around my lips, and when I wash the red skin off the new skin grows back too fast to hide and the new red speaks louder than the words I won't say no matter how much TP I hold over it. I stay in the dark and talk down to the linoleum, hide behind books and under the covers, but the secret climbs up like tomato vines until this slow morning with time to spare and early light. Mama grabs my chin with one hand and spills her coffee cup all over the dining room table with the other. "Rory Dawn, what is wrong with your mouth?"

I want to tell her the truth because her eyes are wet with it anyway, but her hand stays strong as iron around my chin, and the truth will be too loud for the soft clean snow pushing up against the window, too dirty, and so I only tell part of it, the part that she already knows from looking at me, "Just scabs."

It is the stupidest lie I ever told, because I'm crying so hard there's no way I'm honest, and now Mama's crying too. Her eyes shine brown and bright and it's scarier than any screaming fit she's ever thrown. She doesn't cry like me at all, her face doesn't crumple or splotch. Mama sits still and straight and starts talking in a low voice about heaven, hell, and the Hardware Man, and that's when I know I fucked up. I must have said something because she knows.

They grew fast under my fingers that won't stop picking and tearing at skin whose redness reminds me of hot breath and stubble, and then it comes to me that "Just scabs" are the first words I remember saying since school started this year that weren't to Viv or about her, the first words that aren't "I feel sick" at Ms. Hyatt's desk. But maybe I've been talking other times. There must be words I'm losing with all the time that gets swallowed in the dark. Maybe words have been slipping out the whole time, too quiet to hear except in my own mama's ears, and this must be right because she takes my tissue away and hugs me, good and soft and not like metal. She pulls me in like she never does, says words that I've never heard, that I can barely make out through tears and held breath and her voice in my hair.

Mama's "shhhh" sounds clean like cotton and it works away at my apologizing until the morning's quiet again like she likes it, except this morning for the sound of her voice, the drip of her coffee onto the linoleum. "This is my fault." Mama's kisses fall cool on my torn skin and she says it again, "This is all my fault and I'm going to take care of it," and then she says "girlchild." My night name hums in the morning air like the sound of the refrigerator coming on during a scary dream, gives me something to grab onto, something that makes sense, because what she says next sure doesn't. Mama hugs me harder and her words turn hot as prayers on my neck, her words burn into my skin, "You're my heaven and hell-flower, girlchild, and you're gonna grow anyway."

flicker

The hardware man's house is empty. carol is gone and now i stay at grandma's when mama is on swing and grave

the hardware man's house is empty and his truck is gone. and now i go to grandma's during mama's shifts and

there is nothing wrong with me if i just would stop covering my mouth all the time but under my hands there are scabs but the scabs would go away if i just stopped covering my mouth all the time

i did not say good-bye i did not say anything to anyone but can i go to the nurse and grandma has bag balm in a green tin with red roses and ms. hyatt is soft with me when i ask can i go to the nurse and the nurse is soft too takes my hand down from my mouth holds it in hers when the thermometer makes me cry i want to go home

they stay away from the whole swing set because i'm there and i hold one hand over my mouth and swing with the other hand. i rise away

opening my fist she throws away my tissue gives me a new one from the box and i am hot. i will throw up. the thermometer under my tongue. there are phone calls. mama comes and she is worried but she misses work too much misses too much

the hardware man's empty house his truck gone carol in it and

95

me at grandma's when mama is working swing and grave but when the nurse calls mama comes

i will hold my breath i will throw up i will fall down i will pee my pants i'll bite the thermometer in half and eat the glass i'll do whatever nurse needs to pick up the phone and bring mama here.

surge

The lights in my head start staying on long enough for me to see that Mama's forehead is covered with lines and the girls' bathroom is covered with words. The tiles say *i hate Rory D.* in black marker but I don't know what the lines on her face say. I don't know all I've missed, what made the Hardware Man disappear, what I did. When I go pee at school my eyes move from the lock on the door to the words on the wall and when I pull the toilet paper I think I hear the door handle moving. When I go to sleep I dream of the alphabet and black markers, but when I'm awake I don't fucking say anything. I don't fucking say anything to anyone ever, especially not to Viv because I haven't seen her since we went to the playground together to swing, since I must have got her in trouble by making her go to the Truck Stop and she probably doesn't want to be my friend anymore.

School is the same, except it's third grade now, and we are only supposed to write cursive and the letters on the bathroom wall are in cursive too. I write the alphabet in one curling line and my letters bend in a way I recognize, the slash I see in Mama's notes to Ms. Kohler saying, *Rory still isn't up to talking much please understand, thank you.* It's the same slant I see on Grandma's clippings from the *Reno Gazette*. Her angry scratch in the margins: *Can't believe this shit!* and *Who gives a rat's ass?!* My penmanship is pure Hendrix for sure, I bet even my blood runs wrong.

97

The toilet paper rolls and I pull up my pants quick when I see that the letters slipping across the tile, wrapping around faucets and pipes, the letters making the words *i hate Rory D.* are Hendrix letters. The slants and slashes, even the little *i*, are all mine.

stall

/

For years I dream of the bathroom door not locking, of toilets surrounded by panes of glass, toilets in the center of the living room, of dirty stalls occupied by strangers, by couples already intimate, of finding a bathroom only to learn that the bulb is burnt out, there is no door, that it would be a far better choice to just go ahead and piss myself. In waking life I resist all euphemisms, especially the diminutive, the *potty*, the *little girls' room*.

green thumb

Grandma grew things. Whatever the climate wherever she moved, a garden soon followed after her, tomato seeds went down, a fence went up, and on the Calle I was Grandma's Chief Gardener. My Chief Gardener's duties were comprised of deciding which garden hoses felt like snakes to bare feet in the dark pools of slow moving water that puddled in the desert sand too stubborn to swallow it and holding funerals for the birds found dropped dead, exhausted from flying without rest through a land without trees. Discovered by Grandma's rake and shovel, the birds were buried in the dirt beyond the lot's edge and Grandma'd stand still long enough to amen my silent prayer over their cardboard coffins.

Grandma set me loose on all this make believe, but her work was real. She bent her back before its time, pulling weeds and planting seeds. Whatever Grandma got in the way of surplus food and government cheese was supplemented by something fresh from the ground, ground that she coddled and coerced, encouraged and berated, just like she did me.

Grandma could make things grow in the desert climate, she could read the dirt's tells, knew if it would prove barren or rich. She watered in the moonlight, and again just before dawn, sweetening the soil with sheer persistence. Mama inherited that ability too, to make things grow in spite of herself, her gladiolas surprising the teachers at Roscoe Elementary spring after spring, and Mama's and Grandma's children, some of us grew too.

cut off

The Hardware Man had worked a disappearing trick. Once Mama and Grandma got to talking again, she followed a nagging worry she'd had, pulled me from Carol's babysitting shifts, and sent me back to Grandma's, and as suddenly as she did that, the Hardware Man decided to take a little trip of his own. But when he got back, it was Mama's turn to work some magic. She had promised to kill anyone who hurt me, who dared to reach those places kept safe by the double knots in bathing suit string, and she may not have kept that promise to the letter but I'm pretty sure she kept it to the number, because soon after the morning of heaven and hellflowers, the morning the scabs on my face told the tale I couldn't tell, a tale Mama heard clear and true as if both her ears worked perfectly, soon after that, the Hardware Man found himself eighty-sixed. That was the official word, but I'd heard rumors of the truth and I started to put them together.

The word *molestation* and the phrase *sexually abused* are heard once a year around here, in a short presentation given by Mr. Lombroso as he hands out the pamphlets with the hotline number we're supposed to call should anyone *touch us inappropriately*, and for the entire eight minutes of his speech none of us looks each other in the eye. But no one has trouble with phrases like *son of a bitch* and *touched my kid*, and I imagine Mama had no trouble looking the Hardware Man in the eye when he got back and she said them. Our authorities may deal with trespasses in their own way, but the

101

line the Hardware Man crossed is drawn as hard on the Calle as anywhere else. The words carried all the weight of a judge's gavel, especially coming from my mama, and some of that weight was put behind Calle fists. When the Hardware Man was one fist short of requiring an ambulance, the punches stopped, but the hits kept coming. He soon found he'd lost his regular barstool at the Truck Stop, walked into the bar to find silence, his seat taken, his tab run dry, and not just on Mama's shift either, because bad news rolls like tumbleweed through the Calle, silent but sticky. Soon enough none of the bartenders, at the Truck Stop or Hobee's, had what the Hardware Man ordered, if they could remember that he'd ordered at all. The tumbleweed rolled along, and pretty soon after that, the folks down at Ace figured that Sonny could handle the counter by himself. When the Calle took its final turn on him, the man, who was just a man then, with no uniform to hide behind, no counter to look over, no drill bits to catalog, that man used the last speck of sense he had, packed up his home and his daughter, and went to lose himself somewhere else.

It took a long time to sink in. That the Hardware Man's trailer was empty as a keg at closing time, that the sounds that woke me at night were really only the hands of the clock ticking the hours through, that the shapes the shadows took outside my window were really only Mama's gladiolas growing up to meet the desert sun. When I finally understood all that, I took a long, deep breath and stopped hiding my mouth from fear of spilling a secret that was already out.

tattletale

Bird God. Here is another one of your children that got caught in the jaws of the world and shook hard. She's dead, a long time ago it looks like, so you've probably been wondering where she went. All that's left under one wing is pink and bone, things we're not meant to see, Grandma says. Please take her back into your nest and make Bird Heaven stretch ready for her with lots of trees in case her new wings get tired, the ones you're gonna give her because Grandma says you are. I wrapped her in an orange shoebox by the propane tank. It's our last shoebox and I chipped my tooth trying for a perfect bow this time. The string snagged between my front teeth and I pulled too hard. I lost my baby teeth already, so if you could fix it before anyone notices, that way I won't get in trouble and have all the adults popping out their dentures at me asking do I want to look like them. The bow is lopsided but it's tight, waiting for your scissors to undo it and let her free. If it was up to us, we would've let her fly forever, and it's really mean how you do that, let your creatures get torn apart, feathers everywhere, and don't ever send enough shoeboxes, and then make teeth so fragile we can't make things right for saying good-bye. Grandma says you're never supposed to do that, leave a mess for others to clean up, she has a sign above the stove that says YOUR MOTHER DOESN'T WORK HERE and I'm pretty sure this means you too. So if you'll just take this one more bird home, I won't tell my grandma on you.

mirror image

On the night I discovered mirrors, I was at Grandma's in the bedroom of her single-wide Regal, a bedroom I'd shared with one graveyard-shift-abandoned child after another. Mama had been working worried evenings at the Truck Stop, worried because of the quiet that still had such a hold on me, because I should have been getting old enough to watch myself but still seemed to forget how. Because I forgot to walk myself home, or walked myself to the wrong house, to the Hardware Man's empty trailer, pressed my forehead against the windows, and whispered apologies to Carol's shadow, sure as I was that she was getting all the punishment I deserved for not keeping my mouth shut, for not keeping the secret about her bad daddy in the safe, silent dark. Because I'd sit on the porch waiting until Mama found me there and, without saying a word, took me home or to Grandma's. Because Grandma, despite her own record of forgetful tendencies when her gambling hand itched, was once again the best bet for childcare on the Calle, so there I was in her back bedroom, her mirror in my hand, and Timmy was there too, playing with his favorite toy truck on the floor.

The mirror was a red-handled plastic affair, and I watched my face in the square glass, blue eyes, near-white hair, and a closed mouth, no wide red hole, a mouth very closed against the redness that still traced around it from the scabs I had made keeping myself quiet. I was running my tongue over the few scabs left, seeing

which were loosening, and then, suddenly, over my shoulder, little
Timmy. I was surprised that this could happen all at once, my face,
my blue, my blond, and his face too, his lips vibrating with the
noise of his truck's motor. I could see him without turning to look,
so I took a tour through the rest of the room too. The permanent
beds for the temporary kids separated by the nightstand that had
the lamp coming right up through holes in its two levels, the light
switch always too far for one of us to reach without getting out of
bed to turn it off. Above the nightstand I could see the window
whose curtains were always tied open because it faced the empty
back lot. I tried not to look out there at night but the mirror made
me feel brave, so I did. And that's when I saw that someone was
looking in, watching us.

It was a girl with big curls and a lace collar. Viv. She looked different, though, and I saw why, a stiff Girl Scout sash full of patches
ran from her right shoulder to her left hip. I'll never catch up, I
thought, seeing their number, all the different shapes, and how
proud she looked, and then she raised three fingers, her thumb and
pinky joined in her palm, and touched her fingers to her forehead.
When I saluted back she waved at me, and it looked like she was
waving good-bye.

"Viv!" I dropped the mirror and ran to the window, barely
missing knocking over a scared Timmy who'd gotten so used to not
hearing my voice since the Hardware Man left that my scream had
stopped him still. He sat cross-legged on the floor, one hand still
on his truck, its wheels come to a sudden stop on their imaginary
road.

"Is there somebody outside?" he asked me in a quiet voice, a
voice too small to ever power a truck over Grandma's carpet. It was
a voice I recognized for how low it got, like it was getting ready to
crawl under the bed, trying to hide itself and its owner, and as I
looked out the window, trying to see around the reflection of the
light and my face in it, to see a dress running away in the darkness,

a sash's tail flowing behind, I remembered Carol. I thought of how she would've answered Timmy now once she'd caught wind of his fear, how she would have kept scaring him and kept scaring him until he cried with it, just like she used to scare me.

"Nope," I said, making myself sound very sure even though I wasn't. "Just my imagination."

garbage

It's duck duck goosestep till the bell rings: I march from can to can, take the orange peels from today's lunch out of the trash when no one's looking, and drop them one by one on the ground behind me, a trail from swings to slide, monkey bars to water fountain, circle around the tetherball, cross the four square, through dirt and over cement, orange marks the spot. That's how you make things grow, garbage in the ground, it makes dirt strong. Grandma understands the dirt and what's good for it and so do I. And when the Recess Monitors finally see me, because they don't notice me unless I'm taking tests, because they don't notice me unless the alphabet is dancing out of my mouth, my mouth still red like a clown's, like bad lipstick around my lips and no washing it off, they miss the connection. Because they don't like to look at that either. When the Monitors finally see all the orange peels spread out over the white desert dirt of the playground they blow their whistles and ask who did this. But it's too late, there's no way to tell where it began except for the orange smell on my hands but no one gets close enough to know. No one could tell now that it was me.

Now, if anything grows out of the Roscoe playground dirt it'll be because of what Grandma taught me. If the sand won't accept them and the orange peels dry and curl in the sun and blow away, nobody will look at them and think of me 'cause I never get in trouble, because I'm the star student at Roscoe and as long as I can spell and recite, multiply and divide, and comprehend every last word I read, it doesn't matter how quiet I am or how weird I act and I won't get in trouble for anything, not even for *i hate Rory D.* on the bathroom wall. Star student or not, nobody washes that off and nobody corrects it either. There's a difference between trash and trash, that's what Grandma says, and learning which is which is the best education you can get, but nobody ever writes something nice about *Rory D.*, even though I leave a marker there so someone can, so they can add just one *why not*, one reason why anyone shouldn't, and that's because the only friend I've ever had has gone away.

Children run from swings to slide to water fountain on a white dirt playground. Adults blow whistles and point to a trail of orange peels littering the ground. The trail moves in a cursive line and takes the shape of three letters with an exclamation point at the end: *Bye!* The girl with the white-blond hair stands alone by the trash can, orange peels fall from her hand.

revoice

Timmy and I walk to the playground. Timmy's running ahead, pulling his truck along on a string behind him, so he doesn't see an odd patch of green against the desert dirt of the walkway. It's a green, folded-up bill, a one-dollar bill. George Washington's face is wrinkly and his forehead is huge and he's not smiling but I'm not putting him back. I stuff the dollar into my pocket and run after Timmy. When we play on the swings, Timmy holds his truck on his lap and I check my pocket after each new height to make sure the dollar is still there.

When we get back to Grandma's, I go to her bed and try to tell her that I found a dollar. The words stick like they have been, so I hold it out to her but she doesn't understand me. She says, "Timothy, what's this about?" He shrugs and rolls his truck back and forth on his leg. His mom is due any minute to drive down the Calle and take him home. All his attention is on the curve in the road where the next car will appear and I know how that feels, I know that curve well myself, how the mailboxes at that corner will take just the right shape of the car you want, the arms you want behind its wheel, and make you think your waiting is over when it isn't. Timmy's busy. He's not going to speak for me and Grandma knows it. She says, "I'm sorry Rory D., I can't figure this one out."

I look at the hanging baskets over her shoulder, the baskets that hang over her bed. The bottom basket is full of skeins of yarn, crochet hooks, balls of yarn rolled from skein scraps, a word-find puzzle book, the middle basket has onions. I crumple the bill in my hand until it's warm and moist, like a tissue held too long. Grandma picks up the ball of yarn and the hook she laid down when we came in, and I never even guess that she is tricking me, teasing me into reopening my mouth that I've held too quiet for too long. Grandma's been waiting for the right moment, for something worthwhile that I needed to say and couldn't get help with, and I squeeze the dollar tight and say—and I do say, because I can even hear me saying it—"For your money basket, Grandma."

Grandma smiles and opens my fist. I watch as she uncrumples the bill, straightens it smooth, and puts it high up in the top basket next to the decks of cards. The baskets disappear behind her shirt, green and white, soft over bony shoulder, as she leans down, holds me close, and says, "I sure missed hearing that voice, R.D. Don't let it get away again."

the city of words

That night, when Mama's car is the one coming around the curve, and she comes in to get me, Grandma asks if she has time for a quick game of Yahtzee. It's a surprise because Grandma hates playing Yahtzee with Mama, says that Mama is the devil's own daughter when it comes to rolling dice. If they sit down to play anything, it's cards only, because Grandma says she loses enough on the Strip, she should have at least half a chance at home, and it's cards that listen to her best, whisper in her ear about what else is happening in the pack and where the aces are hid.

Mama kisses me on the head but her eyes are already on the game. "I always have time to win," she says. Grandma pulls the old giant clipboard out from the side of the couch that they use for cards and dice, and then, except for the sound of the dice rattling in the cups, of them falling on the board, there's no noise. They really get into it and I really get bored, and find my place in *The Phantom Tollbooth* where Milo and Tock are being arrested by short Officer Shrift.

"How'd they treat you today, Jo?" Grandma asks. By "they" she means the customers at the Truck Stop and by "treat" she means, did anyone try to grab Mama's ass or leave her high and dry tip-wise.

"No highlights, no lowlights, Ma." Mama shakes her cup when

she talks but only rolls the dice out when she pauses. On other nights she tells stories about customers but this isn't like other nights, this is all part of the game, the old one I've been watching and learning since before I can remember. Small talk is how you get into the other guy's head and how he gets into yours and Grandma's an expert at it. Mama ignores her, concentrates on the numbers she needs, mouthing them before each roll. "How'd they treat you around here?" she asks.

"Fair to middling." I can feel Grandma nodding at me even though I'm not looking at them and even though I'm obviously very interested in Milo's adventure and praying there's a tollbooth waiting in my room when I get home. "That one found a dollar on her way to the playground."

Mama's shaking her cup again, hard, like she always does, like she thinks that's how the luck gets in the dice, but when Grandma says this, she stops, even before she rolls them out. Grandma pauses too and I can see the numbers adding up on that other score sheet, the game that's played inside of every game, and I can tell Grandma's winning all of a sudden, whether she rolled any Yahtzees or not, because when she adds, "Told me so herself," Mama puts down her cup with the dice still inside.

The room is quiet until Mama says, "Well aren't you having good luck tonight," but her voice doesn't have that gambler's edge I'm used to hearing. There's a smile in it, and relief, and when she picks up her cup again, she rolls out her dice without another shake, says, "Would you look at that, just what I needed."

On the way home, Mama asks me if I want to talk about anything, like she's been asking me every night, and I don't think I do but then I decide to tell her.

"Viv moved away."

And Mama does something she's never done before. She reaches over and takes my hand and she holds it all the way to our driveway. Her hand is bigger than I think and stronger than it looks but her voice is gentle when she says, "It's hard to let go of a friend, R.D., even when it's for the best. I bet you'll see her again."

scantron

Mama is working some day shifts, and on those mornings not connected to the night before by headache and regret, she leans in my door and says, "Good morning, Sunshine." I'm surprised to hear that word, and even more to feel it. My room is full of the bright morning light that never made its way under the top bunk of Carol's bed, the morning light that rises on the wrong side of Grandma's trailer, and right outside my window I hear Mama as she dumps her coffee grounds and eggshells into the garden, rakes them in, blends them with the dirt and grounds and shells from mornings past.

Mama on days means no more nights away from home, and Mama on days means she can come to all the parent-teacher conferences they want, and do they ever. Bar graphs bleed to the tops of the pages held in Mr. Lombroso's hands, and our gladiolas grow tall in the small run of garden that is on the sunshine side, the morning side, of our trailer. Mama exclaims at the heights of my scores and her flowers, and asks her most honest question, "What does it mean?"

I sit at my desk and feel my cheeks, stinging and hot, while Mr. Lombroso explains the test scores again. *Percentages* and *peculiari-*

ties, these words are about me and they buddy up and crawl across my desk. I touch the tip of my Number Two pencil to their bellies and watch them snap shut like roly-polies do. They are the same gray as roly-polies, like Ticonderoga lead, and I color them in, to hide them, cover them completely so no one will see. I do it without going outside the lines and then I wait for Mama's next question.

There's no explaining the test scores and nothing to do about it. As far as Mama's concerned, my IQ grows right out of the coffee grounds and eggshells tossed into the dirt on the side of our trailer. She's not sure if it's due to her tending, her carelessness, or some joke between God and the school board, but she does her part to keep it going by sending me to my teachers, the principal, and his secretary, with gladiolas wrapped in wet paper towel and tinfoil.

broke

I see my brothers' shadows in the slumped shoulders on barstools, in the muscles of Marc's back as he rides his bike down his driveway and onto the Calle. And what all these boys have in common is that they're gone, moving away, walking away, drinking themselves away. They're not sticking around. The brothers came to visit once, making the trip through the Sierras together to celebrate Bob's twenty-first birthday. Mama was so excited she wore curlers to bed the night before and traded shifts with Pigeon only so she and Grandma could take them all to the Truck Stop anyway, to show them off, and then she got so drunk they had to carry her home.

They weren't in much better shape than she was, and as they tucked her in on the couch I listened to their voices from my bed, where I pretended to be asleep, when the hall light came on and one of their heads popped into the doorway, checking on me. He stood a second and then came to the edge of the bed. "Hey, Sister." I kept my eyes shut but I could tell it was Ronnie because he was the only one who called me that. It was hard to pretend to be asleep with him so close, so I gave up.

"Hey."

"Mom's sleeping on the couch tonight." I didn't figure he'd want to know that this was not a news flash, so I didn't say anything, and he went on, "I just don't want you to worry if she's still there in the morning."

He sounded so tired from driving not just to the Calle that day but all his truck-driving life, so I said, "I heard."

"All right then," he said, and Bob's voice came down the hall, asking if he wanted a beer. "Goodnight, Sister."

Bob asked if I was awake. "Nope, sleeping like a baby," Ronnie answered, and in between beers cracking open, quiet at first, I heard tales that grew louder of how big I'd gotten, how small I used to be, about Santa Cruz and me riding in a kid's seat on the back of Winston's bike long enough for both of us to tumble to the ground and about the time that Ronnie was swinging at golf balls they'd taken from the De Laveaga Golf Course and he'd hit me smack in the eye with one. "My ass was more bruised than Ror's eye when Mom got done with me." I didn't remember any of this and was starting to feel glad, figuring that older brothers are dangerous creatures to have around and I was lucky to be alive. And that part is true. Turns out I was lucky to have been born at all and brothers aren't the only ones who can be dangerous. As the talk turned to Starvation Ridge and the cabin where my brothers first lived, I heard secondhand from Winston how Mama broke down one night, when he was just fourteen, and told him about her episode.

"Episode, that's what she called it," Winston said, and with that one word his voice turns from the good times of bar talk to a man's voice, the voice of the biggest brother with a story to tell. I listened as he retold it, listened like Gene and Ronnie and Bob did too, all of us hearing it for the first time, together and alone, and Mama sleeping through it all, her deaf ear turned to the room. The story swirled like smoke through the house and as I fell asleep I could see the pictures it made, what my brothers might've become if Winston hadn't decided to move them. If they'd stayed with Mama, settled on the Calle, they'd be just four more boys who didn't know what to do with their hands, but they made it out, and now they've got families and food on the table and their teeth are still in their mouths.

a gambling establishment

From the inside of the shop-room door, a sign reminds, SAFETY GOGGLES. Woodshop is life's anteroom for Calle boys, whose next stop will be either the pen or vocational school, the boob tube or Jiffy Lube, where boys like my brothers, but with faces still soft with peach fuzz, will ache their backs for seven bucks an hour and no dental under cars owned by strangers who will sit and read their newspapers in the waiting room, turn their pages, check their watches, and get up to wash the newsprint down the drain. Boys, like Marc, who will never in their lives sit down to table without black under their nails, no matter how red their skin from scrubbing. These boys, who will grow up to work their bones down to nothing for free coffee but no union, are entreated to STAY FOCUSED when working in the shop, and they do. But for all their focus around the lathe and jigsaw, for all their concentration and success with both tongue and groove, they will still go from this class straight back to the working class, will whittle their lives away and wake at night to the memory of the shop teacher's severed finger, how it dirtied the ice that cradled it as he was rushed to the hospital, and how he held on to the bucket himself with his remaining good hand, his finger pointing a warning from its bed of ice now bled pink as morning sky, PAY ATTENTION.

hozomeen mountain

When Mama was fifteen, she started babysitting after school for a lady named Clovie who lived up on Highway 9. Clovie was twenty-two, already with six kids, but this wasn't too much for Mama because if she stayed home after school she would have to take care of her sisters anyway and no pay. At Clovie's, Mama did almost the same work, for money, and most important, got to spend her evenings in a cabin built back from Highway 9 on a westward-facing hilltop of the Santa Cruz Mountains. She would rush up the highway after school, hitchhiking rides from families still sandy from the beach, to get to the cabin in time to see Clovie off to work, to get the kids sitting down to dinner before the sun began to set so she could sit too and watch it sink into the trees that climbed up the hill she never stopped calling Starvation Ridge.

Before long, Clovie's man Gene started coming home early, before Clovie even, and pretty soon Gene was insisting on giving pretty Mama rides home in his rusting Ford truck, rides that curved real slow down the dark side of the mountain and made Mama forget that she was a broken-toothed girl with baby food on her dress, rides that finally ended up in her getting pregnant with my oldest brother, Winston. Sometime after that, Grandma made their wedding happen. (Shotgun-style, I'd always heard, and cliché as it is, I do enjoy the image of Grandma with a shotgun up against one bony shoulder, promising real business with both barrels, a half-smoked Camel hanging out of one side of her mouth, her

119

voice like gravel in a trailer-park playground. Another Calle stereotype born from the real: sometimes you need the threat of buckshot to get a man's feet pointed in the right direction long enough for his head to follow.)

Mama moved up to live in the cabin with Gene at the summit of Highway 9 as fast as Clovie and her brood moved down, with all the cursing that accompanies such changes in circumstance. Winston's little brothers followed hot on his heels, but aside from the moments Gene spent creating his sons, Mama was left with the television for her company and comfort.

By the time Mama was nineteen, she had four children of her own to watch on the mountaintop and it was then that Gene started doing just what he'd done before. His truck crawled up the hill later and later each night, and sometimes when he came home he didn't smell like the ocean at all. This was when Mama, schooled as she was on the melodrama of soap operas, decided nap time had come to the top of the hill.

My brothers were told to lie down and while they were getting quiet, the windows were latched, and the screen door and front door too. And then the stove. And then the gas, turned as easily as the TV's knob during a commercial she couldn't stand. The only thing Mama didn't shut up tight was the oven door, she left that open while she went to the living room to lay herself down.

Nap time had barely begun when my good brothers' bad father pulled his pickup into the driveway, on time for once, with a bucket of fresh fish in the back. Gene lugged the fish onto the porch, but when he found that the screen door wouldn't budge and there was no answer from inside and a strange smell in the air, he pulled the screen door right off the frame, then kicked the door right off its hinges and went right inside. He turned off the oven, opened the windows, and was cleaning the fish before my brothers knew what happened. And that's the only good thing I can say about Gene Hendrix, Sr. He saved my mama's life. But he only saved it once.

a sock to grow a block

I've just blown out the candles on my tenth birthday cake and I'm cutting the first lucky slice when Grandma says the place looks like a baby shower and we must be expecting twins. The streamers are leftovers from the Truck Stop's Easter picnic that Mama brought home and strung up, standing on the chair herself and not letting me help. I recognize the baby blue and pink pastels, but when Mama says, "Don't even joke," I get the feeling the party's over.

"Ice cream," I say, which is what I want to do when I see Mama's jaw setting like that, scream, and I head for the kitchen. Mint chocolate chip is my favorite, and I'm coming back with a new half gallon of it when I hear Mama's voice, my name in it, tight, like she's trying not to cry. I stop, hide myself in the tall grass of the hallway like an Easter egg in our pastel house, and listen.

"She's going to be fine, Jo," Grandma says. "She's going to be a beautiful woman."

"That's the problem."

"You know it's not. If beauty was the problem, all the Ugly Stepsisters would grow up to be Old Maids. You know what the problem is."

I hold my breath because I don't know about Mama, but I for sure do not know what the problem is, and I'm more than ready to hear it. I can't believe any of us actually knows what the problem is and that Grandma might actually spill it right now, right where my Easter egg ears can hear.

"The problem is not treating yourself like you deserve and it's *your* problem, Jo, not R.D.'s. You take every wrong thing on this earth straight to your heart, like it's a sentence on you, everything's your fault." Grandma laughs a little. "Tried to top yourself off over the first man who stepped out on you. Oh darlin'."

"I was a kid, Ma," Mama says.

"Like you're so grown now, Johanna Ruth," and now Grandma really does laugh. "I wouldn't be your age again for anything in the world."

"I'm just afraid that she's going to grow up like me no matter how I try to get out of her way."

"That's the opposite of what she needs. Why don't you chew on that one? Be *in* her way." My fingers are sticking to the ice-cream box that is glittering with frost from the freezer and I'm about to go in when Grandma adds, "And stop blaming yourself. It wasn't your fault. Or if it was yours, then it was mine, the whole Calle's."

Everything's quiet and I wonder what kind of quiet it is. If it's old hatred for the Hardware Man. If it's the old fight about the day Grandma couldn't stop having one more pull on that shiny handle on the Strip and finally won a jackpot for Grandpa Gun when he found me waiting at the school gate alone, regardless of whether our story that day, his and mine, was anything like what Mama remembered of her own. If Mama's ever let that go, I can't tell.

The silence is broken by Mama, though, and she doesn't sound angry, "I can't change it and neither can you, Ma."

"There's the smart kid I raised. Start carrying that bit of wisdom around like you do everything else, would you please?"

Mama laughs, quiet. There's a pause, and I use it to put it all together, that my brothers' story that night was true and not the fairy tale I hoped, what it means that Grandma can laugh about it, and that Mama is afraid for me, and guilty, and holding on to it tight. I'm trying to put it together enough to be cool when I go back in, and that's when Grandma says, "R.D., you can come in now, before the ice cream melts all over the hallway."

I turn the corner, too surprised to not give myself away, but Mama smiles. "My double-digit kid," she says, and pats the seat beside her.

Grandma keeps on, talking now about how we need a new table, "spruce the place up." She moves her hand across the scarred wood. "You should start saving up, Jo. This old thing reminds me of the Santa Cruz house after the fire." She winks at me. "And that, Bird-day Girl, is another story."

gloss

I'm writing a letter to my brothers. I barely know where I'm sending it to, and it almost feels like I don't even know where I'm sending it from. Part of me wants to write to those kids they were on the Ridge, their heads barely out of Mama's oven and being put back in it, and say that Mama's different now and they should come back more often, and say that Mama's different but she still needs saving. But instead I write to them where they are now and say things that come from where I know they want me to be.

Dear Ronnie,

Thank you for the lip gloss you sent for my birthday. I like the chocolate-flavored one the best. I bet Tracy picked it out and I hope you'll tell her I really like it. Mama wrapped it for you with a silver bow and left it for me this morning to open before school. Later on we had cake and ice cream and Grandma came over and she called it my Bird-day about a thousand times. Did she sing Happy Bird-day to you when you were little?

I just wanted to say that I liked your visit and you should come back more often.

Please tell Win and Gene and Bob I said hi when you talk to them because I think you talk a lot to each other. You can always call here too, and talk to me, and I'll take a message for Mama.

Maybe when you come back you'll bring my little cousins. I can babysit while you and Tracy go out. I've read the Child Care section of the <u>Girl Scout Handbook</u> about forty times, it's under "Health and Safety."

Love,
Your sister, R.D.

clipped

THE COURT CALENDAR

Tuesday, March 31, 1970
Superior Court

Joann Ruth Gilbertson, 26, of Santa Cruz, who pleaded guilty to possession of marijuana last October, was sentenced to three years' probation. No fine was imposed, financially speaking, but emotionally, this family will find themselves in the red for generations. This is especially true when considering that the family's hopes of a brighter future went out with the flames that were overtaking their home when the marijuana was found. Why the SCPD showed up during the fire is not clear, but the community is grateful that the police had no other pressing business that evening.

the girl scout laws

The Fourth Amendment hangs from the doors of the scariest houses on the Calle, makes its patriotic protest against unlawful search and unlawful seizure from homes that never came close to lawful in the first place. Homes whose wiring and plumbing are gutted for quick cash from the junkman, whose windows shatter forever against the duct tape that still holds the shards in place, whose inhabitants are known by their burnt fingertips, their bruises, their long sleeves in summer. All that's left inside the houses is the paranoia of the users who haunt them, waiting for the cash that won't come until the next first or fifteenth. These are the folks who tape the Fourth Amendment to the front door believing its promise—*The right of the people to be secure in their persons, houses, papers, and effects*—will keep the police out and their secrets in. These are the folks who think that because a document is sacred it means the police won't read between the lines and decide that the lines obviously being measured out on glass and countertop are enough for probable cause. These versions of the Fourth Amendment are blurry, handwritten, and hard to read, they hang weary from front doors and gates by thumbtack and nail, shudder there and flip in the wind, now against searching, now against seizing, but for all its ink and big ideas, the Fourth Amendment burns just like anything else:

10-14-69 HOME VISIT   HENDRIX, Johanna #310,788

Mrs. Hendrix had telephoned the worker on an
office holiday to report that her house had
caught on fire the night before and when the
police came to the home to investigate the fire,
they discovered marijuana in the home and
arrested Mrs. Hendrix for possession of
narcotics. The worker was as sympathetic as
possible about Mrs. Hendrix's arrest but both
the worker and Mrs. Hendrix had talked about the
use of marijuana on earlier occasions and Mrs.
Hendrix was on notice that this was illegal. She
was quite distressed in her telephone call of
10-13 and the worker did pay a home visit on
10-14. The damage of the fire itself was not so
substantial that the house could not be
lived in.

Mrs. Hendrix described the event of her arrest,
and apparently one policeman accompanied the fire
trucks to the scene of the fire, and while all of
the children were out in the street and the
blaze had been extinguished, the policeman found
some marijuana and a cigarette roller in the
living room. Mrs. Hendrix resisted his attempt
to arrest her and she herself states that she
used some very bad language in resisting the
arrest. He eventually forced her into a patrol
car and she was booked the night of 10-11-69 at
the Santa Cruz City Jail. In her possession at
the time of the arrest were several marijuana
cigarettes found in her purse, which she stated

had been given to her by a hitchhiker who used this gift as a payment for the ride.

Telling stories is an important Calle skill and Mama gets the star. I know this even without V. White making it clear as the black and white on the patrol car that took Mama downtown after her house caught fire and her temper with it. But I also know that whether those stories are true or not doesn't matter once Johnny Law's car is headed to the precinct with you in the back. Right or wrong, once that door is slammed shut, it's hard to open it back up. The Officer made short shrift of the Constitution, and ignoring the devastation on the faces of four little boys standing on a smoky sidewalk, he took their mama away. And she never quite made it back. Despite her creation of a phantom hitchhiker, despite her curses, and despite the promises of the Fourth Amendment, Mama never did escape the damage done to her reputation after taking that ride downtown. Despite the promises of *equal opportunity and protection under the law*, so rich in the air in 1969, that night her arrest record got all shuffled up with her social-services record, and soon the childcare she got so she could go to college was canceled, and with it her courses, and Mama went back to the school of hard knocks.

birds in flight

Between her blackout nights and Alka-Seltzer mornings, life with Mama is a tricky one. Winston Dean's the oldest, which means he holds the record for putting up with it the longest. I was only barely rolling over when Winston turned fifteen, folded Gene Jr., Ronnie, and Bobby under his wing, and set out to find the delinquent fisherman and cast their lines alongside him. Before I was old enough to say don't go, my big brothers had already gotten in their Dodge and gotten out.

The Hendrix Four had their bad daddy, and now they have each other. For them, Mama was a force to be survived, a storm to be weathered, and now she's a post-office box. But ten is too young to pull off fifteen, especially without the benefit of facial hair, and anyway, I don't have any father to run to, delinquent or not. I'm not just passing through here. Mama's all I've got.

tent city

The last weekend of July is Revival Time on the Calle, courtesy of the Lions Club or the Elks or the Kiwanis, or whoever adopts animal names and funny hats most of the year but for one weekend turns their attention to the lost sheep on the wrong side of the tracks. For three nights the Calle's drunks and gamblers, its freaks and creeps, move their sideshow from the Truck Stop and Hobee's to a giant tent set up in the dirt at the end of the asphalt, just downwind from the cesspond that was going to be the Calle de las Flores swimming pool, a hole that was dug but never finished and has since taken on a life of its own.

I always play pool on Revival nights at the table farthest from the dunk tank, farthest because the dunk tank is on the Adults Only side of the tent, because the dunk tank is where Mama always is, in the tank or in the drink, drying off at the bar, climbing back in. For this feat she earns a buck a dunk for the Lions Club White Picket Fence Fund or whatever it is they're collecting for this time. More important than that, she earns the admiration of the Calle men and the envy of the Calle women. The promise of possibly dunking Mama, in her cut-offs and rosy-pink tank top, sells tickets. It's that or her mouth, because Mama can't seem to stop pushing her customers, "Bet you can't," and "Keep dreaming," and all in a voice that the Girl Scouts would find anything but sportsmanlike.

Mama brings the money in, and Mama will go down again and

again to applause and hoots from the Calle men. I choose shots to keep her behind me even if it costs me the game, but when I hear the softball hit its mark and feel the crowd take in its breath, the silent pulling suck before cheering, I turn around, because the sight of Mama underwater never stops being a surprise. Maybe she needs the crowd cheering so she can hear her way up to the air, maybe she needs the warmth of the fools who pool up around her, buy her drinks. She'll sit on the bench without a care, even though there's three feet of water underneath her, that her hair is wrecked, that her mascara has run, and in just seconds she'll stand, the rose in the center of her tank top the only thing not made see-through by the wet. And her smile. If she likes who dunked her, she'll flip him off sweetly, the red nail on her middle finger dripping bright as her voice that says, "Bet you can't do it twice," like she can't wait to do it again, like water's never scared her at all. The tent gets louder, she gets wet, dry, wet again.

And this Revival night is special because, while the Kiwanis think it's to celebrate the new tassels on their hats, the rest of us know this is Grandma's moving away party and there's free barbeque and all the Olympia you can drink. The spotlights bouncing off the kegs make everyone squint, but what's hurting my eyes is seeing Mama and Grandma together, not passing by, not handing shifts off, handing me off, but together, and this makes the night so bright that my eyes start to water. Grandma is leaving the Calle, going back to California, because, she says, "There's gold in them thar hills," even though I don't laugh anymore when she says it. What she really means is that she can't fight the one-armed bandit anymore. If she wants to hold on to whatever she's got left she's going to have to get out of his reach, and what she really means is good-bye.

The whole Calle's brought presents for Grandma, a stack of cardboard boxes, brand-new rolls of packing tape, and more seed packets for her new garden than she'll have room to plant, but

Grandma brought a present for me. She hands me a sheet of twenty-cent stamps and a stack of envelopes. "This is how we're going to stay together," she says, "until you get old enough to get out of here." And I'm looking at my new sheet of stamps, white eagles ready to fly, when the music starts again and dancing feet kick pebbles pinging into the keg behind me. The music's too loud and too fast, "On the Road Again," and when I look up, it's Mama. She's dancing in bare feet, her toes are grey with dirt and her still-damp shirt is getting caked with dust. She grabs Grandma's hands, kisses them both, and says, "Dance with your kid, old woman." Mama's words are all slurs, she's slam-dunked for good, but even so, her feet and Grandma's move in time, raising clouds in the dirt as if they'd danced together every night of their lives. The crowd claps and hollers, moves in closer and closer, until I can't see Grandma's braids flying and Mama's dirty feet dancing, and then I think I hear my name, Mama's voice singing Rory Dawn over and over to the rhythm of Willie's guitar, calling me to come dance, and I want to disappear before I'm made to join them on the floor. I won't last under all those eyes. Jim Beam didn't fill up my dance card and I don't have age to protect me from the burning stares so I sneak out the back where I'm tripped everywhere by extension cords and cables in the dark. They run from inside doublewides and singles, snaking down the Calle to light up the tent whose insides are so loud I can't tell anymore whether that's my name I'm hearing or just the crowd singing along.

I slip over the embankment that surrounds the Calle's cesspond, and when I do, the stamps and envelopes slide out of my fingers. I want to grab them back, close my hands around them and hold on, but there is only this slipping away, soft as Grandma's hand slipping from mine. Her gifts disappear into the dirty water and the desert sun rising over the pond will bake them into the mud.

hit and run

It's like a wildfire after Grandma leaves. Regardless of how little or often they saw each other, Grandma made Mama feel like she belonged here and the feeling was strong enough to keep us close without penning us in, and now Mama's on a hot streak trying to find a man to fill the space left empty. Gray-haired or young, slobby or square, the men warm our house for a night or two, maybe a week, and then they're gone, eighty-sixed from our lives as clear and clean as if what took place between them had stayed at the bar. And usually it's a push, no loss on either side, they come in after I'm in bed, leave before I get up, and I couldn't give less of a shit about any of them. But once in a while one loses his heart and once I think I did too, but never Mama. Her heart stays right in place and it's wham-bam-don't-give-a-damn every single time. Whatever she's got, that thing that can say good-bye like good-byes don't mean anything, I didn't get that. And the glass unicorn with the shiny gold horn and hooves that sits by my bed proves it, proves that I can't let go of things like Mama can. The unicorn is from one of these long-gone men, Martin, and so far, Martin is the only one I miss.

Maybe because he took me on their date to Sizzler and didn't care that I only ate soft serve and cheese, maybe because he won the unicorn in the arcade at Circus Circus after fifteen tries at the Milk Can Toss, was ready to try for fifteen more and wasn't losing his temper along with his money, and maybe because he gave me a giant, hardcover-and-color-illustrated copy of *Alice's Adventures in Wonderland* whose pages turned smooth and new in my hands, Martin is the only one I've wanted to stay.

But not Mama. The afternoon comes when Martin is standing on the doorstep asking where she is and why she hasn't called him back and do I think she'll be home soon, and I want to kick myself for opening the door in the first place. I want to slam it on his stupid, sad face, crawl under the window, and turn up the volume on the TV so I can't hear his next question, I know it's coming. "What happened?" Because if I have to answer that question one more time, I'll scream. I'll scream that I'm only ten and he's a grown-up and if I could understand why Mama does what she does the first thing I'd do is explain her to myself, and I guess he can kind of see that because he starts to cry. His tears soak into the rug, slide across the linoleum and right through my socks, and I feel myself start to grow on those tears. I sprout straight up over him toward the top of the bookshelf, and I keep growing and growing until I'm a giant and he's just a little, tiny boy. My cheek scrapes against the stucco ceiling and I count the moth wings burnt against the light-bulb and look down on him where he's shrunk on the porch, and I wish this was Wonderland because if it was, I would be wearing a clean blue dress and shiny black shoes instead of dirty corduroys and wet socks, and instead of lint in my pockets there'd be cake that said *Eat Me* and I'd nibble on a bit of it now and turn this right around, make me kid-sized again and him a grown man with answers instead of questions and the wherewithal to make her settle down and start coming home to us every night.

finger

My pops's last name wasn't Hendrix but it obviously didn't rate much higher since Mama never took it and I never got it. What I know about him comes from listening at corners to the little talking Mama does with her various cowboys after they've bribed her with the promise of a night's distraction and me with buckets from KFC or boxes of Chinese takeout. The food is always cold after being hauled from downtown to the Calle and is almost as salty as the men who listen to Mama's stories like their night depends on it. What I learn about my pops could fill the front of the paper slip from my fortune cookie with room left on the back for lucky numbers and how to say *So Long* in Chinese but it seems about as likely a version of our past as any.

According to Mama, he was once in the navy, traveled all over, and ever after considered himself a pirate. He was a shaggy man and tattooed but born too late to fully realize his dream of high-seas adventure and, besides, could never muster the hardheartedness necessary to the walk-the-plank tradition. But Mama could, and when she decided she could stay broke without him and without having to wash his socks, it wasn't long before, true to family tradition, we hit the road to Reno. Mama says she knows when to cut her losses, and that is for sure, so I try not to think about what was lost exactly in that good-bye I was too young to say. There are plenty of knees to ride pony on in this town and I figure my own Pops wouldn't have been that different from the rest, coming home too late when he came home at all and passing out with his boots still on. Or maybe I picture him that way because even in my mind he's got one foot out the door. He's listed as Unknown on my birth certificate and all Mama has to say about that is, "The damn fools at the County finally got something right."

slow learner

Halfway through fifth grade, Mr. Lombroso calls Mama to the school to talk to her again. Mama does her hair and wears a blouse and clean blue jeans and Mr. Lombroso wears his patient face and gives me his pen cup. It says *I Heart Bingo* and I want to steal his letter opener that has the twin roaring heads of the Lions Club on its handle. Instead, I sit on the brown, scratchy carpet and write the alphabet once with each of his pens while Mr. Lombroso shows Mama another piece of paper with a bar graph like the Reno skyline and my name at the top. I draw a line of *O*'s, blue-pink-black. He says how glad he is that I'm "feeling better since my sickness," and Mama nods quickly at the lie we both told, all of us told, a story for why I went so quiet through most of third grade so well-crafted it's still remembered almost two years later. Mr. Lombroso talks to her about my amazing percentiles, I connect my *O*'s and make an amazing centipede. The scores, he says, "are an indication of serious college potential."

The only person we know going to college is Alex on *Family Ties*, but Mr. Lombroso sounds so happy that Mama tries to be happy too. That's not how she looks, though, and at the end of all his talking she says, "But what do we do now?" He takes a deep breath and starts over again, using different words that don't sound foreign on Calle soil, that don't darken the room like a cloud of summer mosquitoes, leaving us slapping at air. Finally Mama catches one and holds on. The one that buzzes at the end of this sentence, stinger ready: the Washoe County Spelling Bee.

blue collar

After recess it's ABC order till we get through the door and Harris comes before Hendrix. Stephanie Harris is a little bit bigger than me, a little bit neater, and even if she ever talked to me I wouldn't tell her that I know there's exactly fourteen freckles that march from her red hair and down into the back of her dress. So when Stephanie Harris turns around and says, "I was just wondering, Rory Dawn, does your mom work nights?" I'm so surprised she's even talking to me, I'm so busy trying to feel from the inside if I have any playground dirt on my face, I tell her the truth even though she must already know it because the Calle isn't big enough for career secrets. "At the Truck Stop," I say, and I must be dirty after all because Stephanie crinkles her nose even before I have a chance to count the freckles running across the top of it. She looks past me at Jena-with-one-n, two spots down. "No wonder she has so much time to read the dictionary, Jen. Her mom is a bartender." Jena-with-one-n says, "That's a blue-collar job," and Stephanie laughs, her pretty teeth sparkling. She turns the back of her clean, white collar to me, the tag tucked perfectly inside, fourteen freckles in line, and the whistle sounds our march into class.

swing

Mama wore a bright pink shirt to her job at Circus Circus where she got a job running keno the first months we were here. She hated that shirt because it soaked up all her sweat and cigarette smoke and she hated it because it was the color of carnations given at funerals and after shootings and she hated it because it was part of a uniform and uniforms make the people who wear them disappear. Still, every night those first months, when I was four and she was thirty-four, she put on her uniform and I put on my PJ's so I could get right in bed when she dropped me at Grandma's before heading downtown.

Mama worked graveyard at first because everyone has to start at the bottom and at the bottom is the graveyard shift. Only the most desperate gamblers and drunkards hole up in the casino's twenty-four-hour restaurants, wearing the keno crayons to nubs, marking their same lucky numbers over and over again, handing their tickets and dollars to girls in sheer shirts and miniskirts, or short-shorts and fishnets, depending on the runner's age. Keno runs all night and so do the girls. A new game starts three or four times an hour, and tickets are picked up and run to a booth where they're handed over to women who can't qualify as girls any longer because their varicose veins finally forced them off the floor and into pants, women whose paychecks might have been lost to fallen asses and arches but were saved by their ability to do gambler's math. These ladies fade behind the glass, marking each ticket's crayoned circles over with a stroke of ink before crunching the numbers, deciding the losses, and returning the tickets to the young ones, like my mama was, or was pretending to be, and the young ones run the tickets back across the floor to customers not smart enough to go home after last call. Customers who were drunk when they came in but get more and more sober with each blackened keno ticket and each dollar lost chasing numbers that will surely come up next time. Graveyard is six feet deep, no matter how bright a pink uniform lights up the dead night, and graveyard is where Mama learned to say "Fuck you very much" instead of "Thank you very much," but to say it quick and innocent so that men who were busier studying her keno-runner's legs than studying their tickets weren't sure if they'd just been told off or come on to.

pierce

CURRENT FUNCTIONING   HENDRIX, Johanna #310,788

The four boys attend De Laveaga School where it
is felt all the children have been affected by
the upheavals and divorce in the home. Anonymous
telephone calls have reached the social worker,
reporting there is inadequate supervision for
the children while Mrs. Hendrix is frequently
out of the home. A questionnaire was passed to
the school class, and favorite TV programs were
listed. The selections of the boys showed
preference for shows that appear during the week
at very late hours.

V. White:wr

10-21-69

Some things never change, so if anyone's keeping track of how late
I stay up and what I watch on the tube: I like *M*A*S*H* and *Family
Ties* best. *Family Ties* because the dad's beard is soft like his voice
and the mom's teeth are crooked and she smiles sweet anyway, but
M*A*S*H is my new favorite since Mama had to start back on
nights at the Truck Stop because the money on the night shift got

too hard to pass up. With no one to stop me, I spend a lot of time watching TV, because TV-watching's easier than watching my ownself, and *M*A*S*H* is the only show that stops me from hearing how creaks at the door turn into footsteps, stops me from running to the phone to dial the sounds away, until pretty soon the phone that I've been ringing at the Truck Stop stops being answered altogether.

It's because of Hawkeye. Hawkeye helps me find what I'm looking for when I call and call again to every Calle bar to see when Mama's coming home: belief that everything will be all right. And it isn't because he's the funniest guy on television, or because he's a doctor. It's because even in the dust and the dirt and the cold, Hawkeye doesn't quit. Even when he's up to his elbows in blood, and bombs are falling, and the lights won't stay on, he doesn't walk away. Hawkeye will save your life no matter where you come from or who sent you, no matter what color your uniform is or whether you have a uniform at all.

I don't need a questionnaire about TV time passed around the classroom to understand that my knowing Hawkeye top to bottom means that Mama's mothering isn't exactly by the book. But like Mama says, "Fuck you very much," because at the Truck Stop she doesn't have to wear a uniform. The only pink that blushes in that smoky air comes from her Shirley Temples, which are sugar sweet and full up to the top with maraschino cherries. When it was Grandma's shift, she always pushed plain ginger ales on me, saying, "You carry them cherries around just like swallowed gum," and if that's true, I must be positively full of maraschino cherries, but like "adequate supervision," Mama can't worry much about that. This trailer was bought with bartending money, and the lot under it, and the furniture inside of it, the woodstove that warms us up, and I'm full of cherries and the tip jar is full of silver. A quick pour and a friendly smile feel like a lifesaver to a lot of people. And the Calle is kind of a war zone, the enemy is all around us, the enemy is us. We're so pent up we can't even trust ourselves, let alone each other, and just when you think you're going to get some R&R there's another emergency on the horizon, and to top it all off the food is terrible. But mainly, there's wounded everywhere and that's what the bars are for, to house the wounded. Tending bar is a triage all its own.

the nurture of your emergency

One word for each step. "Don't. Be. Drunk. Don't. Be. Drunk." It only takes 237 rounds to get from the back gate of Roscoe Elementary to the driveway of our house. "Don't. Be . . ." 248 rounds to get to the porch. When I was in fourth grade it took 288. "Don't." I am quiet at the door but the words ring loud in my head, 252 rounds to the recycle bin. It works. Mama hasn't opened her first beer yet. What she has done is brought home a new dining room table. New to us.

The table is dark golden wood and has claw feet and a leaf to make it big enough to have six people eat at once, even though it will only have the two of us ever because Mama's boyfriends don't come over for the purpose of enjoying her cooking. The top is so shiny I can see my reflection and over on the other side, the reflection of Mama's upside-down face. She is happy, beaming a smile that is a huge frown from where I am, watching her in the tabletop, and I am about to smile back when she starts in, without even a hello, without wasting another breath on the new table she must have emptied the tip jar for, and then some.

"When I die, this is yours."

I don't want to watch this old scene in the new tabletop. Another thing that started when Grandma left, Mama's talk of her own leaving and what to do about it. What goes to me when she dies, her wedding ring, the hope chest. What goes to my brothers, her truck, the woodstove. Ashes and papers. I'm so pissed that she's starting in again that when the lightbulb over the new dining room table burns out with a POP! I feel like I caused it.

The table goes blank and I'm unstuck, free to look at Mama's actual face but I'm sick of yelling like I always do, "Shut up, Mama, you are not going to die," sick of whispering, "Mama, please. Please don't go." Instead I say, "It's a nice table, Mom, all right?" and go to get a fresh lightbulb.

"Are you ready?" Mama asks from where she is standing on a chair, one hand on its back, the other on the burnt-out bulb over the new table. I'm right where she wants me, at the phone, holding it with my shoulder, ready to dial 9-1-1 at first sign of electric spark.

I roll my eyes as she stands still, waiting. "Just let me do it," I say.

She tightens her grip on the chair and her forehead is starting to shine. She is afraid of electric shock and heights, even this small height, the height from our plastic dining room chair, and I give up.

"I know our address, Mama, I know what to say. Go ahead."

She takes a deep breath and begins the slow turn of the bulb. It moves and I guess it's the lack of shock that scares her now because she stops and laughs and shakes the tightness out of her hand. She starts turning the bulb again. The room fills with the sound of metal scraping metal and I let the phone slide from my shoulder, place it back in the cradle.

do a good turn daily

At Roscoe, it's easy to tell the Calle kids from the ones who live closer to town. Our pants and pencils are shorter, our homework is handed in with creases from being folded into pockets, not drawn flat and clean from Pee-Chee folders that scream "Wham!" and "I Love Ricky Schroder Forever!" like Stephanie Harris's do. We don't bring cupcakes on our birthdays, and I am the only one, from either side of the tracks, who brings flowers.

Timmy is a Calle kid. His mom might go downtown to get her hair done, but she still only gets as far as the Truck Stop on weekend nights. Timmy's in third grade now but he still brings his toy truck to school and powers it through the dirt by himself every recess. The truck is homemade out of glossy wood that is bolted together so that the cab turns to follow in whatever direction it gets pulled by the yarn tied through its bumper. I wonder which of his mom's boyfriends made him that thing and made promises to come back and play with him again. The promises, I think, must be what give that truck the power to go, and go it does, no matter who makes fun of it or him. I don't tease him, but I don't talk to him either. If Timmy motors near me, I act like we never played together in Grandma's backroom, like I never twisted the grubby blue yarn around my wrist and pulled his truck through her yard.

Timmy and I may be dirty Calle freaks, but we aren't the same kind, or that's what I think until the announcement comes across the speakers about the Spelling Bee finals and my name echoes

148

loud and scratchy through every classroom at Roscoe Elementary. Mrs. Bivings claps but no one else does, and I'm so embarrassed that only teachers like me that when we're let out for recess my face is still hot and I spend a long time at the water fountain waiting for it to cool down. Timmy comes up to me and says, "That's really cool, R.D." He calls me R.D. like we're family or something. "That's so cool about the Spelling Bee," he says.

And before he can motor off, before I even wipe the water that is still dripping down my chin, I've got his truck in my hands. I think I'm going to break it, smash it against the playground's asphalt, but the next thing I know I'm running for the back fence. I can hear Timmy running behind me and his voice is wet and high, "R.D., wait up, wait," but there's no waiting and there's no way for him to catch up, my legs are two grades longer than his. When I get to the chain link, I throw the truck over. It turns end over end, the yarn making crazy loops and curls until it lands in a cloud of sagebrush and dirt on the other side.

Timmy grabs onto the fence and we both stand there gripping the links and breathing hard, looking at his precious truck that is out-of-bounds now till school is out. Even from the fence there's no escaping the voices of Stephanie and Jena-with-one-n singing their idiotic recess songs behind us, I know without looking that they're holding hands and kicking like Harrah's showgirls, "Boys go to Jupiter to get more stupider! Girls go to Mars to get more candy bars!" I'm waiting for Timmy to yell or tell on me, but he just stares at his truck, mouth open, so I keep my eyes on the wooden wheels gleaming in the sun and move my hand down slowly, link by link, until our hands are close enough to touch and my knuckles rub against his. I want to tell him that it didn't break, that it'll still be there after school. I want to tell him that I'm sorry, but then the bell rings and all I do is grab his hand before he can move and hold it, one second, before we go to line up for our classrooms, and neither one of us says a word.

proficiency badge: god's eye

Symbol: *A window framed by curtains yellow and bright as flame*

To earn this badge do four of these activities, the three starred are required.

★1. Steal scraps of yarn from Grandma's lowest basket. Intermediate: Act as if you didn't notice the next knitted surprise she had hidden at the basket's bottom. Advanced: Take yarn in all the colors of the Girl Scout Badges you plan on earning but will never officially receive.

★2. After the Ice Cream Man is gone, search the Calle for used popsicle sticks. Put pairs together in the shape of a cross. Do not wash them. Sugar is Mother Nature's glue.

★3. Wrap the yarn over, under, and around the arms of your popsicle crosses, creating a diamond or "eye" pattern. Make one God's Eye for each badge earned. Intermediate: Award the God's Eyes to yourself in official ceremony. Advanced: Make a short but formal speech of gratitude as you accept your God's-Eye badges.

4. Be ashamed of having made God's Eyes as you grow older and come to realize that they are considered kitsch. Advanced: Stay abreast of what is considered kitsch.

5. When you are older than that, be ashamed of having been ashamed. Intermediate: Begin saving popsicle sticks. Advanced: Award God's Eyes to yourself and others in official ceremony before displaying them proudly in windows and from rearview mirrors.

mayfly

Insects fall under Nature in the *Girl Scout Handbook* and I swallow my fear and try to earn points toward my Insect badge by learning the difference between butterfly and moth antennae, just what is a "true bug," and the work behind collecting live ones to raise. For every one I remove from the dangers of the drain or the broom, there's another putting down stakes behind the toaster, in the corner of the shower, and Mama, who's afraid of everything now since Grandma left, everything but men, is screaming for me to come and kill it. I try to save them, but pushing them around with jars and newspapers only maims them, severs limbs, breaks wings, defeats the purpose, so I start letting them live where they are. I push the toaster closer to the wall, shout "Got it!" loud enough for Mama to hear, move the curtain just so to hide a carefully crafted home, and think of Grandma:

Because it was my Bird-day, Pigeon sent a present. A most unusual gift—a new flyswatter. It is on my wall along with my picture of you. In one corner of this swatter's business end a small hole has been cut & a logo on the handle explains, "Even flies deserve a chance." Think about that!

And think about it, I do. And about how hard it is to believe in chances, but how much harder it is to let that idea go, with Grandma's words lining up so sure and strong in her slanting felt-tip, letter after letter, another lesson in the strength of an old gambler's faith. But if Grandma's right, and there's a chance of slipping through the swatter, if the great hand holding it lets me fly free, it'll mean that I got the opening and everyone else got left behind. Mama already feels so alone here with Grandma gone that I can't see leaving either of them, no matter how flat our future.

trigger

After I began my correspondence with Grandma, she begged me to stop addressing her as Grandma Gun, a name I'd held on to for its fierceness and fight and written boldly across the front of every envelope I sent her way. That is, until the letter came that called him, in capital letters and haggard underline, a Vile Memory. Grandma underlined her maiden name for me too, saying she'd rather be a Crumb than a Gun any day. So old Gun was retired, Grandma Crumb it was, and the real why of it all was never discussed. However many we send, letters don't keep Grandma close enough for Mama, though, and the secrets they try to share long-distance spill out in her sleep, Vile Memories with them. They race up my arms as I tuck her in, surge under my skin, creep the way bugs do. Insects started out as Mama's fear but like her wedding ring and the hope chest, it's one of those things I'm inheriting. Her dyslexia saved her from what she couldn't face straight on, but I don't have any trouble reading Gun's swarming of Mama at night.

word jumble

Make as many words as you can using letters from the following word. Do not repeat a letter if it is not repeated in the original word. (You have one childhood to complete this portion of the test.)

INSECT

dyslexikx

Mama's first car was a pretty blue Chevy Corvair bought for her by her first and only husband, Gene. Gene got it thinking to free himself from having to drive her on all the errands a family needs done, but in the end the Corvair freed him from a lot more than errand-running, and Mama too. The key to that freedom was hidden just under the front seat, close enough that Mama's curious fingers brushed against it when she went to slide the seat forward on her first drive down from their cabin on a Santa Cruz mountain and into town. Tucked under the seat, forgotten by the car's previous owner, was a library book, and for Mama it was long overdue.

When everything you need to know to get through life is written on box tops, recipe cards, and collection notices, reading through a whole book seems like a mighty waste of time, especially if you have problems with letters, like Mama does. "They go ass-backwards," she says, "and if I'm tired they don't stay still at all." But if you just got your first car and you're feeling around for the seat lever and find *Desolation Angels* instead, the beautiful people on its cover so lazily entwined, well, that's the type of experience that can turn your head around.

And when Mama finally drove her Corvair down the mountain again, to the library this time to return that book, she would've paid the fine too if they'd asked her, guilty as she was for all the

155

time she'd kept it, the days and nights spent while her boys ran wild and the ironing heaped high, each page a headache of squinting until the words clicked like the tumbler in a lock and the page could finally be turned with a surprised and secret hallelujah. After dropping that first book through the library's return slot, she showed her new driver's license, filled out a form, and left with two more Kerouac books under her arm, the orange card of the Santa Cruz Public Library in her wallet, her name having been misspelled by the librarian across the front, Mrs. Joann R. Hendrikx.

Before long, Mrs. Hendrikx's library card number, No. 21431, was stamped on the inside of every Kerouac book on the Santa Cruz Library's shelves. I don't know how much credit old Jack deserves for the fire his writing lit in Mama's life. There's such a thing as the right book at the right time, and for Mama and many others, Kerouac's was it. Whether he liked it or not there was something like a revolution going on as his books came out, especially in Santa Cruz where Tibetan prayer flags still wave more proudly than Old Glory. Every revolution needs a voice, and in 1969 Kerouac's voice was loud enough to catch the ear of a recent divorcée who, though not well-bred, was getting well-read, and thinking about a revolution of her own.

Letters still refuse to behave for Mama but she doesn't let that get in her way. There are books on our shelves to prove it, not dusty candles and dime-store glass won at Circus Circus, not pictures of family and plaques offering the same advice from one trailer to the next: *Don't talk to me until I've had my coffee. I'm not a slow cook / I'm not a fast cook / I'm a half-fast cook. God grant me patience and I want it right now.* When the men Mama brings home see the names lining our shelves, Kerouac and Kesey, Gilman and Ginsberg, the traveling Buddha tucked in a corner, they tend to catch their breath and quiet a bit, not sure whether they stumbled into a library somehow or drank themselves clear through to Sunday and woke up at church. Santa Cruz couldn't be further behind us and all our books come from the Salvation Army now, because Carson County, Nevada, officials haven't yet seen fit to shuttle the bookmobile this far up the 395, but Mama's old Santa Cruz Public Library card doesn't leave her wallet. No. 21431 was her ticket out, once, and she needs the reminder.

spelling bee

I win a set of *Academic American Encyclopedias* and two wide-winged trophies. I win a trip to Kmart's parking-lot sale to get a new dress to wear to the statewide competition and I win the weird, confused pride of my mama. Mama says she has no spelling smarts but she finds her way through all our books, fights her way through all the letters, so that only leaves her saying it to make it true, just like Grandma said. She says that I didn't get it from her, couldn't have, a mix-up at the hospital, she laughs, embarrassed. By me. It's like I was never a part of her, like I hatched out of a spider egg instead, crawled out of somebody else's anthill, like I flew out of a honeycomb with a dictionary under my arm. Mama acts like I don't belong to her anymore. And her saying it is just making that true too. And that's just fine. Because I never feel, I never ever feel, like Mama belongs to me. The only place I feel like myself and the only person who treats me normal is Mrs. Reddick, the librarian. In her library I can sit and let all the words leap and run and I don't have to pretend it's harder than it is to have them make sense, like I do at home. Mrs. Reddick doesn't have a thing to say about how fast I read or where it comes from or why. I come in, she smiles and nods, I smile and nod, and then I open my book and read until the bell. That's it. I'm no alien and nobody's miracle, I'm just a reader right at home.

The only time it was ever different was right after the Hardware Man left, when I came back to school the first day after the snow-

158

storm that left Mama and me alone with my secrets, the first day after the fist-storm that followed. Mrs. Reddick's smile that recess took longer in coming than usual. Her eyes held on to mine for such a long time, I felt like I was reading them too and what they said, about worry and being glad I was there, felt too loud for a library. The look was enough to make a librarian say "Shhhh!" and Mrs. Reddick must have scolded herself, because she bent her head politely to her stacks and I sat down.

an illustrated book about birds

Mrs. Buchanan finds me in the library at recess. She's got something in a paper bag that I know is from the drugstore because of the way the brown paper creases tight. Mrs. Buchanan is Mr. Lombroso's secretary and her clothes never get tired of fitting, never wrinkle, and circles never show up under her arms. She's so pretty that, the first time they met, Mama said, "I wonder what *Mrs.* Lombroso thinks about that." When she sits in the chair next to me her perfume is so sweet that my mouth goes dry and she says, "Principal Lombroso asked me to check on your preparations for the Spelling Bee final. Have you been looking through the dictionary?"

I wish I was sitting closer to the big dictionary and not right here in plain sight with *Flowers for Algernon* in my hand, but I can at least see it from here. I'm figuring out that whatever's in the bag must be for me, maybe a notebook, and I want a notebook, so I look hard at the dictionary and say, "Yes, I've been looking at it." Mrs. Reddick is hovering an aisle away in Bird Watching and I know she's listening because no one ever messes around in Bird Watching so there can't be anything to tidy up there. But out of the corner of my eye I can see she doesn't flinch at what she knows is my giant lie, and Mrs. Buchanan must believe me, because she sounds relieved. "That's very good. You can't spend too much time with it, dear. Do you have one at home?" We do, of course, it's at Mama's elbow, but I wonder if I said no would Mrs. Buchanan come back tomorrow with a dictionary hidden in a paper bag so the other kids wouldn't know I was her new favorite? I imagine her house, off the Calle, with deep carpets that show the vacuum lines and a bedroom ready for a little girl of her own, with a brass headboard and too many pillows in the shapes of circles and hearts, pillows that don't do anything but take up space. I want to say I don't have one so she'll invite me home after school to use hers, and bring me hot chocolate while I turn the pages, but I figure one lie is enough and from the corner of my eye I can see Mrs. Reddick, a drawing of a hummingbird flutters from the cover of the book she's holding, and I tell the truth.

"Of course you do, dear," Mrs. Buchanan says, smiling, and pushes the bag across the table at me. "Mr. Lombroso and I wanted you to have these for the Championship." I'm excited when she says "these," because that means two notebooks or a pocket dictionary and a notebook, maybe, and I reach into the bag, but what's inside doesn't have anything to do with spelling. What's inside is a pair of tights in a package that says "Perfect Girl Seamless." There's a picture of a perfect girl on the front. She's leaning against white steps that lead up to nothing and her legs are an unnatural and seamless shade of cream that doesn't match the rest of her at all. Mrs. Buchanan says, "Do you know how to put these on?" and I don't, but before I have to admit it, Mrs. Reddick drops the book she's been holding, the hummingbird crashes on the counter, and she comes over to our table and says to Mrs. Buchanan in a way that only librarians know how to do, in a whisper that sounds like it came over the loudspeaker straight from the principal's office, "This is a library, not a dressing room, Diane."

Mrs. Buchanan's face goes red, and for the first time I notice how silly she looks in the kid-sized chair. She gets up and I notice that her legs are an odd shade of cream that doesn't match the rest of her at all, but her earrings and bracelet and necklace that catch and shine in the fluorescent light do all match, gold squares hugging into each other. If I lived at her house I'd probably have to go around matching stuff all day, the sheets to the pillowcases, the towels to the washcloths, and she probably doesn't have a dictionary, anyway, because there's something improper about a dictionary, the way it stays open to the last thing you didn't know, there's nothing seamless about that, nothing perfect. So I match my tone to Mrs. Buchanan's perfume and say sweetly, "Thank you very much."

We listen to Mrs. Buchanan's heels clicking at a proper pace toward her office, and when the sweet library silence returns, Mrs. Reddick picks up the copy of *Flowers for Algernon* I was reading before Mrs. Buchanan came in and looks at its cover.

"This book is often banned in libraries." She hands it back to me, open to my page. "There are many ways to define intelligence, Ms. Hendrix," she says, as she puts the package of Perfect Girl Seamless tights back inside their brown paper bag, "and most of them, as you are already discovering, are completely inadequate."

shell

Under Arts and Crafts in the *Girl Scout Handbook*, there is a section on design and the symbol on its proficiency badge is a conventionalized flower. Not an orchid, sultry and moist, not a gladiola, ruffled and tall, but a *conventionalized* flower, petals uniform and polite. If you've never had the pleasure, a conventionalized flower is one so sturdy and dull the weeds don't even try to choke it dry, preferring instead to fight with the beauties at the other end of the yard. The Girl Scouts and V. White have one thing in common: they like to play it safe. V. White didn't ask how far Mama *could* go, just how far a person like Mama *has* to go. She was only interested in the shortest distance between Mama being on welfare and earning enough to stay broke without welfare's help, or better yet, figuring out why Mama didn't stay married just enough to keep off the dole altogether. As far as V. White was concerned, there was no reason for the County to send Mama to college and be made smart when, for less time and less money, she could go to vocational school and be made useful. I doubt it's what V. White had in mind, but Mama does make herself useful now, pulling taps and making change, and her collar is as blue as my eyes.

Girl Scouts learn useful stuff. Proficiency badges can be earned in all kinds of fields. Except academic. There's nothing in the *Handbook*'s index under Science or History, no listings for English or Math, but there's loads to do under Arts and Crafts and there's much good work to be accomplished in, say, Child Care or Nutrition, that would lead the dedicated Girl Scout into just the type of vocational training program V. White mentions in her initial report on Mama.

In the *Handbook*'s section on design, under "How to Begin," there are three simple drawings of a bird in a row and the question: *Do you want to use a bird in your design?* I hadn't thought of it, but if I'm here to learn how to draw and if all they're offering is birds, my answer to this question, like my mama's answer to the question, *Would you like to earn a certificate that would bring you financial independence?* is: you bet your sweet ass I do. I do want to use a bird in my design.

Pigeon and her husband started the Truck Stop when the Calle de las Flores was just a twinkling rhinestone in some developer's eye and they kept the bar going even after the major plans for building up the area fell apart. But when her husband made one too many trips across the pavement to tip a waitress working at Hobee's, Pigeon took a trip down to the courthouse before her husband had time to cross back again.

"Birds are hatched from eggs and are always egg-shaped." That's Girl Scout advice for drawing birds. You start by drawing the egg and from there it's easy to draw the rest. In the *Handbook*'s examples, the first bird is only an egg, the next, an egg with a head. The third bird has legs and feet and feathers.

✳✳✳

Pigeon filed for divorce and hocked her wedding ring to pay for new locks on the doors and cash drawer of the Truck Stop, with a little left over for new vinyl to cover its barstools. "That's something I liked about Jo right away," she tells me, "she wasn't one of those fool women who toss their ring into the Truckee and cry poor me. I could tell right off, Jo was smart enough to make use of what God gave her and hold on to whatever else she picked up along the way." Pigeon got over her husband, but she could never get over all the engagement rings thrown by shortsighted divorcées to the bottom of the Truckee, the rings' glimmer lost on the river's trout. The wedding ring Mama still insisted on wearing made sense to Pigeon, and she may have been the only one on the Calle who took its meaning. Pigeon wanted someone she could trust not to run off with the first good old boy who tipped regular. While Mama may have been looking for a good time, by the time we got to the Calle she had all the jewelry she needed and more than enough of husbands.

Draw an egg, the *Handbook* says, or model an egg-shaped piece of clay, and "hatch out" a bird. I look through the Birds from Every Continent section in the encyclopedia, searching for one kind whose body doesn't look like an egg, upright or sideways, but from loon to blue jay, ostrich to starling, all their shapes agree. Take this one to the bank: birds are hatched from eggs and are always egg-shaped. Maybe there's no escaping the shape that molds you, no getting around how you got started even if you do break out. I haven't found a mirror yet that doesn't reflect the curves of the Calle back at me, my dirty ways, my fragile teeth and bad skin, my hands that won't stop picking at themselves. The Girl Scouts win again. And maybe V. White does too. Except for one thing. Wings are born from that shape. They don't come from any other.

the state

It's the final round of the statewide competition and I get
A-L-I-M-E-N-T-A-R-Y
and then I get
H-A-L-F-P-E-N-N-Y
but I don't have any time for their subtle homonyms and sneaky,
silent *l*'s and *f*'s, because all the while I'm just thinking about my
new dress. Not just new-to-me, but new-brand-new with orange
flowers and ruffly sleeves and a price tag I had to cut off with scissors. I'm going to wear it for school pictures and make double sure
that none of its frills turn upside down like last year's Salvation
Army special, or the years before, when my pigtails hurt and I was
scared of the flash.

There is only one more word to go, and I look out at Mama,
small in the crowd of sweater sets that swarm around her where she
sits straight in her best jeans and a new blouse she spent forty-five
minutes ironing, a world record in our house, and still she went on
to do my hair without cursing and only pulled once. Mama sits tall
like everyone else but her face is the only one here that looks how
mine feels, on picture day or any other. Like maybe she's in the
wrong place. And when the Pronouncer says my last word, I feel an
insect curl in my throat and the auditorium goes quiet until she
asks, "Would you like the word used in a sentence? Perhaps?" and
I nod, mouth dumb but eyes smart, eyes on Mama.

The words chase around the walls of the auditorium but I don't follow them because I'm thinking about Mama's sentence. Mama's life. How she never talks about how she reads all the time because she's never had a breath to spare for feeling proud of herself, and now that I'm here, she never will. Mama's already read up to *Ech-Fa* in the *Academic American Encyclopedias* I won and haven't barely opened yet, except to write *Rory D. Hendrix* on the inside cover of each volume with the gold and maroon pen Mr. Lombroso gave me for getting to the State Championship. At least that's what he said, but I know it's for getting Roscoe Elementary School out of the *Reno Gazette*'s police blotter for once and onto the front page for that same once, even if it was at the bottom. Mr. Lombroso got a raise and I got a pen. The brand-new pen made my name feel brand-new even though I could tell Mama recognized her curls in my *R*'s and *y*'s and *D.*'s by the way her smile pressed tight over her teeth.

It's the same way she's smiling right now, trying to remind me that they're waiting, that all these put-together moms and orthographic judges are waiting on my next breath, for the insect in my throat to unfurl itself and fly out in the shape of the correct letters.

I pronounce the word right but I spell it

O-U-T-L-I-A-R

because wrong is the only way they let you off the stage in this game. If I spell it right, they're going to applaud and their applause will be polite and "cold as a witch's tit," like Grandma would say on winter mornings when the coffee's still brewing. They'll send me on to the next level, and the next level will take me farther away, in dresses I don't have, on days off Mama won't get. Wrong is my ticket home and I'm cashing it in. And they let me off the stage, their sorry applause rings against the sorry blood in my ears as I run to Mama's arms and they wrap around me and hold me tight.

loser

The prize for losing the Spelling Bee is that Mama takes us out to dinner. I'm thinking she's going to make a speech but all she says is "Don't forget your book" when we pull into the Sizzler parking lot and that is exactly all I want to hear. Reading during dinner means it's business as usual. At least Mama pretends it is, she does give me too-long looks over the top of *Pocahontas*, some history-type book bought in the checkout aisle at the Save-Rite, but I drink bottomless Cokes, eat cherry tomatoes and sunflower seeds, read *I Am the Cheese*, and don't look back.

We come to Sizzler sometimes on paydays, but never dressed up, and the lady whose job it is to take away our dirty plates must think our outfits mean payday for her, because she doesn't try to get me to reuse my silverware. Mama and I read straight through dinner, only stopping for our trips to the salad bar and my two trips to the soft-serve counter, and then I read all the way home, my finger holding my place in the dark stretches between streetlights.

I'm still reading as we enter the house and don't stop until Mama comes out of the bathroom, her clothes changed and a bottle of nail polish in her hand. Identical bottles of red nail polish line the back of the toilet for every day before work, when she paints her nails a new coat of perfect red, but tonight she's not scheduled to work and I make a face at her going-out jeans. Mama exhales smoke through her nose and leans down to give me a kiss, but the click of the metal ball in the bottle that she has begun shaking, the clicking that signals her preparing to leave, turns my head. "You look like a dragon when you do that," I say, bending the spine of my book backwards until it cracks, but I'm glad that she's going. For once, I want to be alone. I smile at her and say, "Don't kill any villagers tonight."

partners

We are not making turkeys this year," Mrs. Croxton says. Because we're moving on to Roscoe Junior High next year, and to prepare us, our Thanksgiving project will be to write our first research reports. She says this as she walks around our circle of desks and hands out the red, white, and blue cards stacked in her hands. Written on every card is one of our "glorious constitutional amendments," and I get a blue card with letters in big red marker that reads "Fourteenth Amendment: Equal Protection of the Law." Mrs. Croxton says that we are to take our amendments to the library where Mrs. Reddick is waiting to help us find the books we'll need to become research experts. And then Mrs. Croxton says that, because there are only twenty-six amendments and there are thirty-two of us, she repeated some of her favorite of our many freedoms and that we can work in partners if we want, and as soon as she says this, the classroom bursts into sound and waving and running. From across the circle, I see Stephanie Harris got the Fourteenth Amendment too and I'm caught up in the rush. I walk over to her and even start to ask if she wants to work together, but she looks past me, at her best friend forever, Jena-with-one-n, and they laugh together at the very same second and their laughter crawls up my spine and turns my shoulders so fast I'm already back in my seat before Stephanie can say "No thanks, Rory D." I sit through the burn of my blush and read over and over the words—*Equal Protection of the Law*—where they blur on my desk.

At the library I wait, last in line, so that I can have more time with Mrs. Reddick, and when Stephanie gets her stack of books, she turns to me and says, "Guess you'll have to wait till I'm done." I couldn't care less about waiting and I hand my card to Mrs. Reddick, but for the first time I can remember, she doesn't smile. My card bends in her grip as her eyes follow Stephanie to where she sits next to Jena-with-one-n, dumping her books on the floor. Then Mrs. Reddick looks me up and down and her eyes slow at the let-out hem of my pants, at the yarn that curls around my ponytail, and she says, "I know just what you need, Ms. Hendrix," and, "Why don't you sit here at my desk." And I do. I sit behind her big wooden desk while Mrs. Reddick starts bringing me book after book from the teachers' section of the library. Each time she brings one she pulls her glasses up from where they hang on a thick silver chain and reads through the index, then she opens it up to pages that tell stories of Brown versus Board of Education of Topeka, of Roe versus Wade. I'm thinking about how I've heard those names on Grandma's lips, in the same angry breath as "privacy" and mumbles about who's "running this show," and then I see, in the next book Mrs. Reddick sets down, a name I know myself. The name is Vivian Buck. The ones beside it are Emma and Carrie, and next to those, the word: *feebleminded.* Mama was right. I did find her again, and after spending all this time alone, finding my best friend right there on page 237 feels like an exclamation point in my heart. Stephanie can have her BFF with her one lousy *n*, I've got mine and I'm not letting her go this time. I take a finely sharpened pencil out of Mrs. Reddick's pink-and-white-flowered pencil jar, turn over my blue amendment card, and start to write.

reading comprehension

Read the following passage carefully, then answer the question. (You have fifteen minutes to complete this portion of the test.)

DEGENERATION: THE CASE OF *BUCK V. BELL*

"Feebleminded" is one of those terms, like "debutante" or "Social Security," that is not often used in seriousness anymore. In the recent past, however, feebleminded was considered scientific and used to describe the congenital deficit of stupidity. In 1927 the phrase was given the judicial seal of approval when the U.S. Supreme Court decided that the gene pool should be safeguarded from those considered feebleminded via forcible sterilization.

The Bucks are perhaps the most famous feebleminded Americans, the poster family for all the term was made to encompass: promiscuity and addiction, both encouraged by a stupidity able to withstand any effort at edification. Emma Buck was the first in that family to be officially declared mentally defective, and in 1920 she was remanded to the Virginia Colony for Epileptics and Feebleminded. Emma's daughter Carrie, along with her other children, had been sent to live with foster parents. In the foster home there was an uncle or cousin who couldn't resist Carrie's sad orphan eyes, and before long he took to muffling her sobs with kisses and comforting her deep into the night. Soon, Carrie became pregnant.

Carrie's pregnancy established her promiscuity, which proved what science had already hypothesized: Carrie was loose, just like her feebleminded, alcoholic mother, and therefore feeblemindedness, promiscuity, and heredity must go hand in hand in hand. Carrie's child, Vivian Buck, was left with Carrie's foster parents to raise, and in 1924 Carrie was sent to the Colony to join Emma. Once there, Carrie Buck won national attention when her case, which argued that her right to bear any future children was a constitutional one, was lost before the Supreme Court by Irving Whitehead, a board member of the same institution that wished to sterilize her. Supreme Court Chief Justice Oliver W. Holmes determined that in light of the traits she had obviously inherited from her mother, and certainly passed on to her daughter, forcible sterilization was a legal act in the best interest of all.

Based on Holmes's decision, upwards of fifty thousand intellectual defectives were forcibly and legally sterilized before the practice was quietly brought to an end in the 1970s. Sometimes the feebleminded were not informed of what was about to be done or had been done, being told instead that an operation was needed to cure appendicitis or female trouble or was simply for their own good. Sometimes they lived the rest of their feebleminded existence without ever knowing why they failed to bear children, and sometimes they learned the truth after decades of fruitlessness and failed marriages.

Which statements are true according to the passage?
A) *Science, governments, and your doctor should be trusted.*
B) *"Comforting her deep into the night" is a euphemism for sneaking candy.*
C) *The ugliest phrase used in this passage is "female."*
D) *Bad things really do come in threes.*

sunrise

The Government's official opinion of Carrie Buck, as given by Mr. Justice Oliver Wendell Holmes, is stated clearly in his argument's conclusion to *Buck v. Bell, 274 U.S. 200*: "three generations of imbeciles are enough." And so Carrie was sterilized without anyone thinking she needed to be told. The thinking on Mr. Holmes's part was that if members of the white race behaved in undesirable ways, these behaviors would creep into the upper classes like weeds, root down deep, and put the choke on the delicate hybrids growing up around them. Holmes was so concerned about the importance of good breeding even the Fourteenth Amendment didn't give him pause. He well understood the amendment's notion of one's right to one's own body and to one's own plans, and hopes, and dreams for that body, but he just couldn't see what that unalienable human right had to do with the obvious defective before him.

Since Mr. Justice had no problem bringing his gavel down on Carrie, if he could swing that thing so blind in her case, it's hard for me to believe he would have had any problem hammering it home in the case of *Hendrix v.*, had we been in her position. What with all of the begetting and begotten, the Hendrixes have proved themselves biblically fertile; but without the need to see our unions made holy or legal in the eyes of the Lord or the law, we're just as guilty of the sins Carrie Buck was tried for as she was. The drinking and drugging haven't helped our reputation much either, but without the drinking the unions hardly stand a chance of being consummated, and without the drugs I might've come into the world in the usual way; with a name that didn't sound like a screaming sunrise and a father listed as someone other than Unknown on my birth certificate.

A pregnant Mama named me Rory Dawn because she was tripping on acid, and me with her, I guess, and I watched through her peaking skin the sun rising over the Pacific, blasting hot pink with warning through the window of her ocean-facing San Francisco hotel room, a bearded gentleman asleep on the bed behind her. Old Holmes was long dead by then, and Mama was so concerned with her own history in the making I don't think she gave any thought to that bit of history we've lost, the dark marriage of genetics and class, the miscarriage of children and justice that took place less than fifty years before. If she had, she might never have seen me through to my first roar.

Whatever decisions Mama weighed, whatever history she lost, never learned, or plain ignored, that morning she trained her eyes to the promise of the sun rising over the Pacific and gave me a glimpse of the potential that Holmes, via willful ignorance or a simple lack of psychotropic drugs, could never see to believe: how short the distance is between the haves and the have-nots, the cans and cannots, how where you're born is sometimes all that separates a sure thing from a long shot. These possibilities tangled in my umbilical cord, warmed to the pink hint of dawn and the thrum of Mama's voice as it echoed right into my newly forming bones, Mama promising a threat I inherited, words as familiar as my own skin, "Pink sky at morning, sailor, take warning." The Fourteenth Amendment's flag flies in triumph for Roe and Brown but it still hangs at half-mast in the case of *Buck v.* and I can't let that stand. I may not have been born captain of this boat, but I was born to rock it.

The American Dream

This classic cocktail has gone through a few changes since its first manifestation. The original recipe called for equal parts ambition and sweat with apple-peel spiral for garnish. The signature characteristic of the modern American Dream creatively substitutes a nearly perilous belief in oneself in the place of the historical apple peel.

Equal parts sweat and heedless disregard
Dash of bitters
Lucky twist

Stir. Strain. Garnish.

VARIATION: For an ultra-dry American Dream, substitute an actual fortune for the twist of good fortune usually required.

average

When I get my report back, Mrs. Croxton's red pen has pushed too hard into the paper to tell me that I should have "stayed focused on the big picture of the Fourteenth Amendment" and not let myself "get sidetracked." Mrs. Croxton "expected more from me." Where usually I hide my papers so no one can see the plusses and stars and A's, I have a new reason to turn my paper over today. I fold it into tiny squares and wait forever for the bell to ring.

When I get home I wait until after Mama's asleep to take my paper out and read it again, the details of Holmes's decision, of Vivian Buck's life, how he couldn't see that the equal protection the Fourteenth Amendment promises applied to Viv and Carrie's lives, to their futures, that it applied to their bodies too, and how this probably means the Fourteenth Amendment just isn't going to be enough to count on for the rest of us either. And then I read Mrs. Croxton's notes again, about how the "unfortunate mistakes" made in the case of the Bucks aren't important enough to overshadow "the victories that have been won for the underprivileged." Mrs. Croxton wanted pretty pages about how far we've come since slavery, not ratty truths about what work awaits us with other groups still deemed less than human, and her final comment, "This Report Is Not On Target," hangs right over the angry, empty claw of my very first C. Average.

I've been waiting for this since the Spelling Bee, waiting to fade into the background, to end the challenge I didn't mean to present to the Roscoe teachers and their empty expectations of the Calle kids. I finally got the grade I thought would make me feel right at home, only now it feels like there's nowhere worth belonging to anyway. I ball the report up but I'm afraid of Mama finding it if I throw it in the trash, so I open the stove door quietly and toss it onto the ash and embers. It smolders there, the facts of Viv's life lost in the smoke.

family ties

Roscoe Junior High has always been on the brink of Nevada's Great Basin and now it is officially on the brink of something else: at risk. This isn't new, but the term is, borrowed from the medical field when the vocabulary usually used to describe populations notorious for their stupidity and stubborn will exhausted itself. So now there's a special term to describe us, but we're just as invisible as before, maybe more so. The only real risk that concerns the teachers and administrators at Roscoe is the risk of having to do their jobs. They aren't worried about us slipping through the cracks. They are the cracks. Fading into the background after losing Roscoe's chance at the Spelling Bee was easy. The idea that Calle kids might have some potential hiding in our dirty creases gave them a scare. It's not like they work on commission. So when I lost at State and then proved myself hopeless with my report on the Bucks, we all breathed a sigh of relief and returned to the regularly scheduled failure. Now I toss my homework in the ditch on my way home from school like everyone else, and after late nights, I tiptoe past Mama's still-sleeping body but bang the kitchen cupboards to beat the band when the milk carton's empty and the Wheaties are gone. There's no making college plans when you can't make breakfast plans. Wake up Mama with Alka-Seltzer, plop, plop, fizz, fizz, it don't matter who the president is. It's morning again in America.

the great chains of being

If I drew pictures of the Calle families, this is what they would look like. Not family trees, more like weeds really, just as simple, stubborn, and unwanted:

Buck	Hendrix
Emma$_d$	Shirley Rose
|	|
Carrie$_d$	Johanna Ruth
|	|
Vivian$_d$	Rory Dawn

The little *d*'s that bud on some folks' trees are round and ripe as *d*aughters but here they all hang withered to let us know who's *d*ied. Some folks, like Viv, have long been dead but make appearances for the living, and some, like Mama, can't seem to get that little *d* added fast enough, *d*eaf to those they'll leave behin*d*.

The Bucks live in history books written far from the Calle, and their lives were spent in the wet Old South, not the dry Old West, and in the Roaring '20s not the boring '80s, but I count them as neighbors. As family, because Viv came through for me when no one else could and because our families' patterns are so alike we might've been run off on the very same Singer. This way: Vivian belonged to Carrie, Carrie belonged to Emma, and all three of them belonged to the State. The Bucks, like the Hendrixes, were passed from the arms of one social service agency to another their whole lives. By virtue of being a Buck, Vivian's fate was predetermined, and by virtue of that, the fate that comes with a name, Viv was just like me. Except that her story's told and mine isn't. The Bucks' history lies flat and fading between the pages of my *Academic American Encyclopedia*, only paper and ink now, but the Hendrix story isn't finished yet.

Buck and Hendrix. We are each three generations, a trifecta, but don't lay your money down just yet. Both our mamas' and grandmas' races have already been run and while Viv and I barrel along, neck and neck, we are still third-generation bastards surely on the road to whoredom. Dirty, white, and poor. We're pure as the driven slush.

There's no way out of the trap of your own blood, short of spilling it, science said so and Justice Holmes agreed. Regardless of Viv's small achievement, that she made the honor roll the spring before her death when the wisteria that grows strong and stubborn in Southern gardens was just blooming, by that time, science and the State had already moved on to other business and no one noticed either her accomplishment or her passing. Viv died from a stomach ailment when she was eight years old, or so the encyclopedia tells me. Its authors are as unalarmed by this piece of information as by all the atrocities that have come before and spare no surprise for what comes after: that at the publication of the fourth edition of the *Academic American*, in 1984, Holmes's ruling still had not been officially overturned. The encyclopedia may have learned not to hold its breath for justice, but I'm getting blue in the face.

Viv and I share this history. These are our mothers and the beliefs that touch us and the words that judge us and like the entries in the encyclopedia, there's no keeping just the good parts and separating the rest. Mothers and grandmothers might align Viv and me but the Man does the rest. We're like shoes tied tight together and thrown over electrical wire; every pulse going through that wire goes right through us. The rain makes us heavy the same way, the sun dries us out and then hardens us, cracks us where we used to bend, the wind sends us swinging. The only way to get free, of our families—of this place—is to tear our very selves apart, to say good-bye and go on alone, so we hang here and wait for the County to send someone out to clean us up.

I'm pretty sure that Viv never got to be a real Girl Scout, coming as she did from a place like the Calle, where patches are for mending and oaths are only muttered underneath the breath. But if Vivian Buck, feebleminded daughter of a feebleminded daughter, herself the product of feebleminded stock, if that girl had lived, she'd be in my troop, and with three fingers raised in Promise we'd show them just what the third generation can do.

Some of the things that belong to Scouts and Guides of the whole world are: the Promise, the Laws, and the Handshake. These fall under the heading "International Guiding and Scouting," and the distinction must be made and notice taken that excepting these basic tenets, we Girl Scouts of the United States, even those wasting away troopless in the deserts of Reno, are very different from them, the Scouts of the Philippines and Czechoslovakia, for example, who await our used books and toys, and those who, if the *Handbook*'s illustrations are on-their-honor true, lie abed in sanitariums in France. Excepting the oath taken and the laws followed, excepting the ways we must partner for safety, the way Viv partnered with me, the miracle of our palms creasing each into each as we looked both ways before crossing Calle streets, excepting this brief sisterhood of our held hands, complications of which the *Handbook* never discusses, one thing is made perfectly clear: there is no lasting fellowship here. We connect through its pages but close the book and we become just what we were. Alone.

This, from the Intermediate Program of the *Girl Scout Handbook*. Girl Scout being among the most impermanent of titles, its fleeting description marches across the page with no concern for its mortality. Capital letters stand stiff and proud like the future leaders they beckon, through chapters on propriety and promise only to be abandoned on page 504 under the heading "How to Become a Senior Girl Scout." We are left suddenly in uniforms grown too small, our wrists stretching from their cuffs as bare as the page.

Girl Scout describes child, female, who holds the book first with both hands. Hands that are too small to bend the spine and crease the page alone, they bear the weight together until, grown up now, one hand is enlisted to twirling wisps of hair around an index finger, while its mate loses her place against the margins when the shouts from the boys' camp filter in through the trees. She raises her eyes from the page, better to hear the deep newness of Boy Scouts' voices promising they'll grow up to be Eagles, and her voice, her words and oaths and promises, to "do a good turn daily" and "do my duty to God and Country," fade into the past while she moves forward on a future Eagle Scout's arm. These girls' sashes will be put away and preserved for the next generation, or sold at thrift stores, or used to tie up curtains at daybreak, to flood sunshine into a room and reveal dust as it floats by the hard-earned patch that says "Cookie Champ 1977," the patch that says "Eager Reader." These specks call the once-future leaders to attention. Hands that imagined finer tools and greater work, young hands that saluted straight, now curl to their housework. Broom and duster are secured by hands flecked with gemstone and silver, spotted with age, and worn with the care of little scouts of their own.

tour of duty

Mama allowed me to be in danger, and the kind she most feared. As she would say, and she would say sadly, and to no one named Jack, "That's the fact, Jack." It's confusing and outrageous and it is a fact and it's starting to make sense. It makes sense because Mama was in danger once too, and when she was, she lost true north. Maybe if she'd gotten help, joined a Girl Scout troop for example, memorized the "Compasses, finding directions without" section in the *Handbook*, it wouldn't have taken her so long, too long, to get it back.

Mama's compass spins round and round, lands Mama in strange lands, and me with her. Santa Cruz for starters, Reno next, we might land anywhere. Next stop, Vietnam, where the mopeds and motorbikes run like salmon up a stream and the riders wear few helmets and there are fewer upheld laws and even fewer traffic lights. The families ride together along with their groceries and livestock and Mama and I ride right beside them, just like Grandma did, all her daughters on board. It's dangerous to ride without a helmet, a little girl on the handlebars, but it's the only way we know how to get around. How can Mama explain to me what safety looks like? How does a woman raised on the handlebars of a speeding moped explain a seatbelt? It seemed a safe perch to Mama, the handlebars of the moped of our life, her compass spinning like the speedometer as we barreled through.

But what do I know about Vietnam and its circus of bikes, anyway? What old copy of *National Geographic* did I pull that out of? It's just that I'm starting to realize how in the dark Mama was, so much so that even if she'd known that Carol left me alone with the Hardware Man, she wouldn't have stopped it. She looked at Carol, who seemed okay, who put on the same show I tried to, and saw exactly what she never saw in herself, confidence, and so she thought Carol's dad a safe dad, just like everyone on the Calle did. Until they didn't. Until they realized the stranger bringing the danger was right next door, a man they hardly knew they didn't know. Mama couldn't read the signs, not by herself, her sign-reader got jammed up way too long ago, and instead of hating her for it, this tour of Vietnam is my attempt at finding a light to forgive her by.

word problem

A man with 9 fingers has 4 times as many male grandchildren as female, and 3 times as much regret. The amount of regret is equal to the number of times his shoulder has been dislocated from the recoil of a shotgun blast at 21 foot-pounds of force per bullet multiplied by the number of times he has been called a dirtbag to his face. Given the number of shell casings littering the bedroom floor and the number of shells ready in the box, how many of his original 4 daughters have been deafened by gunshot?

(Show all of your work.)

A) The jar holds 5 times as many pennies as nickels.

B) Each team will need to load 12 bags of dirt.

C) The mother will purchase 22.4 yards of gingham fabric.

D) The shotgun blast echoes for at least 3 generations.

triangle

I never did talk to Mama about the Hardware Man. He had his threats: *don't fucking say anything to anyone ever.* She had hers: *I'll kill anyone who tries.* And they ran together: *I'll fucking kill anyone who tries to say anything to anyone ever.* Even after he was gone, I kept my mouth shut. The ember tip of her cigarette was too bright. I was stuck between a scary place and a scary place, so I just waited it out, waited for questions that never came, and after it was all over, except in my dreams, I tried to forget. But one night, long after the Hardware Man and Carol had gone, after I started watching my ownself, tucking myself in when Mama worked nights, on one of the rare nights off that she stayed home, Mama comes into the living room where I'm watching *Family Ties* and stands there smoking until a commercial. And then she turns down the volume and speaks his name, and through the wail of blood in my ears I hear her say that he, "Uncle—" the blood rushes through my ears so that parts of what she says are drowned in the roar, but I hear there was a fall off a slick roof, something about rain and the roll of duct tape he'd been using to fix a leak falling down after him. And the uncle who isn't an uncle is paralyzed from the neck down.

She doesn't take her eyes from the TV and I don't take my eyes from her hand, steady, her fingers wrapped around a can of warm Diet Pepsi, Jim Beam inside. Don't take my eyes from her cigarette angling between her fingers, from her wedding ring sparkling in the blues and grays from our quiet set.

"Oh," I say, because someone's got to say something, still watching the fire burning down to the filter, wondering how it all holds together, how the ashes build on nothing, cling to nothing except maybe being warm and next to each other.

She stands that way until the commercials end, then she taps the ash off into her palm, takes a drag. "Carol is all right," she says, pausing, "now. Thought you'd want to know." When she says Carol's name, I can hear it just fine, there's no blood rushing, no fear, and it hits me that I do want to know that she's okay. I've wanted to know this for a long time and my voice is thick when I say, "Thanks, Ma." It's my first and only thanks for all Mama did, no matter how late she did it, and for all of us she did it for, herself too. The thanks feels like a wave pushing out of me, and I watch it wash over her where she stands, looking at me now.

"Sleep good," she says then, and turns the volume back up. The Keaton family's voices fill the space between us as she walks down the hallway to her room, almost drowning her "girlchild" as she closes her door. And I decide I don't need a TV mom to sing me to sleep tonight after all, so I turn off the television and go to bed.

lesson plan

Whatever satisfaction Mama got about seeing my fake uncle's taillights disappear off the Calle, she didn't rejoice about his accident. There's no room for rejoicing here. The only tiny bit of joy comes from the reassurance that, no matter how flawed the County is, or how blind the judgments of the State, there is a greater order at work, and like a pink morning sky, you can bet it means business. Mama did her best, short of bringing the County down around our ears, and trusted the rest of the work to the karmic police, the only force that's ever done us any good. Everything that goes around on the Calle makes its way back, and waits at your door for you to trip over and break your fool neck. That's why the Hardware Man's accident doesn't surprise Mama or me. Leaving the Calle won't get you free of justice. It found the Hardware Man, wherever he went, and taught him the lesson he had coming. Taught him what it feels like to lie very, very still.

hypotenoose

If the lengths of any two sides of a right triangle are known, the length of the third side can be found. Let *ABC* represent a right triangle, with the right angle located at *B*. The altitude from point *B* to point *A* is as tall as the shadow of a man and a new triangle is created. If the legs of the new triangle are 12 inches long and 9 inches long, and a little girl is ½ the height of the man's shadow at midday, use the Pythagorean theorem to answer the following question: What is taking place inside of this triangle?
(Show all of your work.)

A) *Things like this do not happen in right triangles.*
B) *The darkness is overcome by degrees.*
C) *Roots are being squared.*
D) *The little girl will.*

will

"When I die this is yours," Mama says, and this is her hope chest and this is her wedding ring and this is the bookcase with Gibran and Kerouac way at the top. And she says, "I want to be cremated," and cremated means her body isn't buried, because she says, "Save the land for the cows." She says she wants her ash body taken to California and spread out on Starvation Ridge, because "God knows I deserve that," and Starvation Ridge is where my brothers were born and might have died, and her with them, because she tried once, and failed, obviously, or we wouldn't be here talking about her regrets. And deserve means she expects to be punished for that death wish forever, and by her nonstop talking about it, it seems like it can't come fast enough to suit her. And finally, she says, "No machines," and by machines she means at the hospital to keep her body alive, because the whole point of all this is that Mama is going to die.

This is her list, I know it by heart, I have for years now, but I don't know what brings on the telling or how to make her stop. Too much pink in a sunset or breeze through a window, too much beer in her blood or not enough, and Mama's eyes roll like the reels on a slot machine. Come up sevens and our house is afire with cursing, come up tilt and she curls up quiet to sleep, come up like headlights over a mountain range and Mama has one foot in the grave and this list on her lips, because you can't just give death your number and expect him not to call. Just like anyone else she ever flirted with, Mama knows he'll be back.

nails, how to drive

It's time we had wall-to-wall carpeting, Sunshine," Mama says over her coffee cup one morning, and since there isn't a man worth a good shag within a hammer's throw of the Calle any more, she's going to do it her damn self.

I never thought anything was wrong with the old linoleum-carpet mix, but Mama's got this big idea, and her big idea means that half the living room is now particle board, and that every pay-day I have to go with her to the Carpet Store to guarantee the single-mom sympathy discount. The Carpet Store stinks like plastic and stings my nose, my nose that's out of joint already because of the tightness of Mama's jeans. She always wears her tightest jeans to the Carpet Store in case the single-mom routine doesn't work, and because she knows when she does the Carpet Man'll be sure to watch her leave, which means he'll be even more sure to have a pile of samples saved for her the next time we come and might even throw in a few for free. The one time I do try to balk, I tell her that I had a rough day at school, turn on *The People's Court*, and throw myself on the couch in my best impersonation of teenagers from television. The Honorable Judge Joseph A. Wapner is just taking his seat when Mama slings her purse over one shoulder and turns off the TV.

"Put your shoes back on, R.D."

I've already seen this episode, the one about the missing bird, but I keep up with my Carpet Store rebellion. "What's the big

195

deal? You don't need my help. It's not like we're choosing what pieces we get or something. We get whatever's left."

Her purse slides off her shoulder a second before she pulls it back up. She holds it firmly there and says in a voice that's firm too, one I know better than to argue with, "That's the thing, Rory Dawn, we always choose what we get. Now I suggest you choose to get your goddamn shoes on and let's go."

We bring home another stack of carpet pieces, outdated samples and remnants too short to sell, different-colored, different-styled, different-lengthed, and different-piled, and Mama gets down to it. She cuts the squares precise, the colors blending against the mortar and brick under the woodstove, against the frame of the door, and she mumbles through the nails she holds in her lips, murmurs about this green and that yellow while she hammers them in, and never after that does she ask for my help or advice, and I don't offer anyway, and as the paydays roll past, our wall-to-wall becomes a reality.

Six pay stubs later and our living room is carpeted in the brightest blues, golds, and violets, patterned and deep. As she's packing up her tools, Mama is all smiles and says, "See if you can pick a favorite, R.D. I bet you can't." I don't think to question this until I walk across it in bare feet, sink into the plush of this square and that. I don't think to question this until I imagine doing it myself, deciding what goes with which and making it permanent, believing in my choices enough to pound them in with a hammer.

border crossing

Mama has a red truck with an Indian name, and we drive it west through the desert and then up through the trees that separate us from Grandma's new digs on the California side of the law. Mama only drinks her soda warm since she got the dentures that make her gums sensitive to hot and cold, and so I ride with my bare feet on the dashboard and a can of warm RC between my legs and try to get used to the idea that we are going somewhere. We cross the border that separates the State of Nevada from the State of California just about the time that the sun is fully up behind us, because she says she wanted to hit the road early, arrive early, and get a drink early, but really it's because Grandma is "sick and needs visiting," and that's news to me too. Mama decided we were taking this trip last night, got down a suitcase I didn't even know we had, told me to get to filling it with the cribbage board, a carton of cigarettes, and pop for the road, and if all of that wasn't surprising enough, she says she wants to tell me a story about her life.

The story begins with the splash of desert insects against our windshield, and it's about a drive Mama took to Mexico when my brothers were small and Mama a single mother trying to make her ends meet. I don't know if the story's true because I know from my perch on the Truck Stop's fridge that Mama "tells a tale to make a sale" and that "flapping lips get the tips." I don't know how much of what she says actually took place in the Santa Cruz Mountains that rise over our past and how much got added in the Calle bars that make up our present. But, because this story will be mine someday, like Mama's hope chest and all the answers that aren't in it, I'm keeping it.

Mama met someone who knew someone. This someone needed help getting several kilos of marijuana over the Mexico-California border and Mama said she would do it. And though she had recently been arrested for the coincidence of having marijuana cigarettes in her roller on the same night that her house happened to catch fire, and though she was on probation and had four children to think about, she said she would do it because she could make a cool grand, and in 1971, according to Mama and even the State of California, a thousand dollars went a lot further than Mama's welfare dime or her dime bags could ever dream of going, so she decided she would go very far for a chance to get it.

Mama had a boyfriend then, a man who, to hear her tell it, never wore a shirt but always wore work boots under tight-fitting jeans, a man who was hard at work at a construction site when she first saw him and whistled at him from the window of her old blue Corvair, got his phone number, and as she drove away, told her sons to sit up from where they were hiding in the backseat and help her memorize it. This man, shirtless and booted, took Mama as far as San Luis Obispo where he left her with the Driver of a Hollowed-Out Van.

The Driver of the Hollowed-Out Van was not fond of women and wanted nothing to do with Mama in particular. She wasn't a pro, she was too young and probably too pretty to be useful, plus she chain-smoked and she never smiled, like she doesn't smile when she tells this story now, like she would never learn to smile, even with teeth that cost as much as our trailer. But Mama gets in the

Van anyway, and because I can't know which parts of what she says are truth and which are made up to make the trees roll more quickly down the highway, I try to fit the story into pictures I can recognize. The Van becomes Grandma's red van with the beanbag ashtray on the console the summer it swarmed with bees, and the Van is a van that was parked outside the Hardware Man's trailer that I have both not enough and too many memories of, dark as the taste of cigarette ash. And Mama and the Driver sit in the front of this Van and they make it across the border into Mexico, make it across easy.

Mama and the Driver arrive in the city in Mexico where they're supposed to pick up the bundles that will fill up the hollow parts of the Van that has become Grandma's Ford Supervan inside my head as we roll along toward her house, except now, the Van is parking on a dusty Mexican street and the beanbag ashtray in the center of the console is filled with cigarette butts and the windows are alive with bees.

The Driver leaves Mama in a marketplace to consider chicles and leather goods, and when he returns he tells her to go on up the stairs of the little hotel he has just come down from and meet the man who is in charge of the Mexican side of this deal. And Mama, who is nervous but not too much, steps it up when she sees the lines of sweat that are creasing the very bald top of the Driver's head. She has just bought puppets for my brothers, four banditos, and is considering a señorita for each, but she hands them over to the Driver. The puppets' strings tangle as he clutches them to his chest and tells her to be careful.

Mama goes up the stairs alone. The door is open, and there is a fan spinning and a bed in the center of the room with no spread but a white fitted sheet and a white top sheet, and in between, a fat man sitting in a white tank top. The Fat Man is leaning against the pillows of the bed, which are bunched up and crowded behind his back, and there are two more men in the room, one who answers the door and another who sits across from the door and holds the gun.

The Fat Man in the bed tells Mama to sit down and points to a chair backed up to the wall behind her and she imagines the Driver sitting in that same chair and the blossoms of sweat that tickled his forehead. Mama wishes she had a cigarette in real life and in the story, and in the cab of our Indian truck she pushes in the lighter. I watch it glowing red in her hand and the way she takes a pull, as if it was her first cigarette of the day instead of her third, and it makes me think that maybe this story is true after all.

The Fat Man pulls his knees up and looks at her across the top of them, surveys Mama where she sits in the straight-backed chair. He looks her over, then he speaks. And the words that come out of his stranger's mouth aren't foreign, they're American, American as baseball, and Mama knows them well: Winston Dean. Eugene Thomas. Ronald Joseph. Robert Dylan. Hendrix. Hendrix. Hendrix. Hendrix. My four big brothers who never felt so close as I feel them now, hanging by threads in the Driver's hands on the street below. At the end of this list he says just one more thing.

"Do you understand?"

I drain my cola and look at Mama's face. She says it again, "Do you understand?" and I realize she's asking me, and I tell her I do.

Mama says she still doesn't know how he knew the names of her four sons, my four brothers, who, if you do the division as the Fat Man does, with an eye on profits and losses, are only worth a mere $250 apiece in 1970s scratch. She keeps her eyes on the road, and says, "He was holding the sheet and each time he said a name he pulled the sheet up a little more over his knees. By the time he asked me if I understood, I could see his balls, his cock, everything."

My face goes hot and I roll down the window and hang my head out. I lean back against the door, the highway wind in my hair, and watch the side-view mirror until those words are whipped out by the wind, disappear into Mama's blind spot, and blow away down the highway.

Back in the Van and a few miles before the U.S. border, Mama pulls a muumuu over her head and folds down the purple frill that circles the muumuu's neckline, tucks the straps of her tank top underneath it and reveals one shoulder, the other, both, as the Driver slows behind the line of cars waiting for inspection. This is the reason Mama's on this trip. This is her part to play. She covers her mouth before slipping her hand into her pocket, her hand that is holding the set of teeth that have cost her so much, and she is silent until they reach the guard shack. The guard was bored before they pulled up, tired of inspecting striped serapes and terra-cotta fountains for contraband. He would've liked to investigate a big sled like this from dashboard to fender, and certainly would've been willing to pass the time with a pretty, bare-shouldered girl caught up in the pleasure of a man in uniform, but his mood changes once Mama, who never in my entire life smiled with her mouth open, offers him a smile that is wide as the noonday sun. He can't help but shiver at the smooth, wet gums shining back at him, and motions with his gun to the guardhouse to hurry up and let this Van go right on through the gate, free and legal.

redemption value

Maybe that was the one time Mama smiled crazy, smiled wide. Maybe shame won't let you smile with your mouth like a lantern until you know that your sons' safety rides on you making it past inspection and you see flashes of blinding white sheet and smell the shock of a stranger's sex in a hot Mexican hotel room.

I want to see that smile now, and so I say, "That's pretty cool, Mama," but she barely laughs.

"I don't know about cool, R.D. I don't know what, but when we'd made it through safe and we're parting ways, the Driver shook my hand. He said he'd work with me again anytime. I was proud of that, I don't know about the rest of it."

And that's about where Mama's story ends. My RC can is empty, our windshield is yellow with bugs, but Mama's not adding on a moral here. She lets her entire story of strength and guts and crazy risk fade in the rearview mirror, like telling it was nothing more than a way to pass the time. She leaves me to make up my own moral, so I do. Forget her telling tales for sales, I'm a liar for hire and I learned from the best.

My ending is as sweet as a crisp stack of hundred-dollar bills, and begins with Mama putting her dentures back in her mouth and pulling off the muumuu. As she does, she catches herself in the Van's side mirror. When she sees her face there, she opens her mouth and smiles a big, wide-open smile, and her store-bought teeth are as straight and sure and welcoming as the white lines of the freeway rushing her toward home.

sunset

Grandma is sick. We sit all day in the front room of her trailer while the trains roll through the trees, just like the letters she's sent back to the Calle promised they would. Mama and her play rummy, then cribbage, while I roll skeins of yarn into balls so they won't snag when Grandma uses them to make her afghans or her toys or whatever she's making now. There's no asking her about her health because the cards are out of the box, pulling all of her attention, spades and clubs working at her like magnets, diamonds and hearts full of the promise of their names. The talk around the table is regular gambler stuff, bravado from the loser, "Come on, double or nothing," even though they're only playing for beer tabs. Teasing when the win is too easily come by, "Do you smell skunk, Ror? I swear I just got a whiff of skunk."

There's no need to ask her if she's sick, anyway. Her body tells the story. She's lost so much weight she put three pillows on her chair, "to save my bony ass," she says, and her hair has fallen out in patches. The exertion from shuffling the cards sends her coughing all through the next hand until finally Mama says, "You want me to shuffle?" But Grandma's only answer is, "You'd like that, wouldn't you? Now shut it and cut it."

When all the yarn is rolled, I get up and dig through the newspapers and crochet hooks and scraps of fabric that have been pushed together on the table to make way for the card games.

204

When I find Grandma's brush and I start on her hair, I'm surprised when she doesn't shoo me away. Instead she says, "Let's make this the last game, Jo," and beats Mama easily before sweeping the beer tabs back into their jar. "We don't want to miss the sunset," she says. Then, "Help me to the couch, R.D., and open that door wide."

The couch is Grandma's bed still, and Mama moves the blankets over to make room. With the door open, we have a view of the Sierras and the sun setting on their ridges. I'm sitting on the floor, leaning against Grandma's knees, and it's a good thing because when Grandma says, "Pink sky at night, sailor's delight," she can't see me roll my eyes.

The saying may be as old as the hills but tonight it feels brand-new. The sun settles into the mountaintops so gently through the frame of Grandma's screen door you'd think the Sierras were made to be seen just this way: on shag carpet with bony knees behind, cigarette smoke and the sound of shuffling cards fading in the air.

It feels like the whole town's followed the sun over the mountain, it's so quiet. We sit until the sky's almost all returned to blue. Grandma finally breaks the silence in the near dark, "You'll have a good ride home, Jo." And when Mama answers, "So will you, Ma," I don't wonder what she means.

calle de las flores

Mama is quiet on the way home and I miss the sound of her voice and the excitement of her Mexico story from the morning, but when I turn to her I see by her eyes that she's thinking about Grandma, and before I know what I'm doing, I reach for her hand that, for once, isn't smoking, but sitting on her lap.

"It's hard to say good-bye, Mama, you told me that once." I squeeze her hand and remember the rest of it, Mama's advice to me about Viv. "You'll see her again."

She squeezes my hand back, our hands almost the same size now. "What a wise young lady I raised," she says, and holds on until we get on the dark highway. "Keep your eyes open for deer," she says then, and I try to keep my eyes open, look for the frozen reflection of our headlights in eyes peering from the shoulder, but the window is cool underneath my cheek, and before long I'm back on the Calle, only instead of trailers, we all live in huts.

The streets are still dirty, the pond still grows frogs and shopping carts and still smells. A retired taxidermist is in Grandma's space now, his work on display at the Truck Stop. From the same barstools where they stare at Mama's tits, the glassy-eyed drunks stare across the bar at a glassy-eyed moose, their future reflected. But in the dream, Grandma is dead and men are coming to confiscate her bones. The men are officials. Grandma's bones are contraband.

The men will be in uniform and they will be fearsome. I am sitting outside of my shack on Calle de las Flores and I'm afraid. Grandma's bones are in a bag tied to my belt loop. It is a small bag. They are small bones. Like those of a bird. I am feeling Grandma's bones through the cloth of the bag, I have already rubbed them smooth as river stones, but my fingers continue to seek the sharpest edges, to wear them down, and they are doing this when I see the fearsome, official drab of uniforms approaching through the dust being kicked up on the Calle.

I run for the pond and roll down the embankment, hoping the dust on the Calle confuses the men long enough to let me set Grandma free. I make a small hollow in the muddy shore and push the bag inside just before the men holler at me to stay where I am, hands above my head. I'm about to do as they say when the sound of gravel crunching under tires wakes me to the familiar sight of our headlights against the Nobility and Mama saying, "Come on, girlchild, let's get you into bed."

highlight

When I grab the wire I can't keep my eyes open and my body shakes and my teeth chatter and then I let go of the fence somehow, or maybe it lets go of me, and I slam on the ground, and when I open my eyes, there is Horse. He is finally noticing me—me, a person with feelings who needs some attention. And I think I understand him better, I think I understand him better every day. And I think we are making friends.

I am lying on the far side of the pond, as far as I can go from the Calle without permission. Not that Mama wouldn't give it, but getting permission would mean asking for it so I skip it. I'm lying under the fading roar of an engine. I open my eyes in time to see a plane disappearing, the white trail it leaves behind, and watch as the streak separates into the rattle of chain link. It could only be Marc and DeShawn jumping over the fence into the field. I don't even have to look. I know it's them because they are just too strong, or too dumb maybe, to do anything quiet. But I look anyway and I see I'm right. Even from here I can see DeShawn's belly button poking out from underneath the T-shirt he's too big for and Marc, still too small in his dad's leather jacket. And right behind them, a girl. She is new on the Calle, and her clothes are new too, and I think we could be in the same grade, but her hair has highlights and her earrings are long and shiny and her eyes are frosty. We don't have any classes together but she hangs out with Marc and DeShawn at breaks, distant at the edge of the quad, huddling by the exit, ready to be the first ones out. She made friends fast. She did not try to make friends with me.

The three of them walk straight for me, laughing, but I flatten against the ground, hold my breath, they aren't after me, I say, not after me. When they stop, barely a trailer's length away, the girl disappears into the weeds at Marc's feet, and then he disappears too, and then I'm sure I'm right. They've already got something to do.

The three of us lie on the ground together, in the same dirt and the same weeds, but they don't even know I'm here. Not just here in the field, but here, on the Calle. They don't think about me like I think about them, like I think about Marc. How the hair under his arms curls weird and silky like the *c* at the end of his name. Like how DeShawn keeps watch, stays standing, his eyes on the trailers behind the chain link, watching for the flash of cars coming up the Calle, and about how I keep watch too, on him and Horse and sky, everywhere but on the two in the dirt below him. How the streaks of white from the planes pick up pieces of each other and leave pieces behind, how they take the shape of zippers and hooks and unbuttoned flies.

When the quiet is over and they've started talking again, the clouds are all broken into mist and DeShawn laughs without looking down, he never looks down, he makes their privacy happen even when they don't need it anymore. He laughs in the direction of Marc's trailer and then there is Marc, standing suddenly beside him, pounding him on the back, throwing punches at the air. The girl stands up too. She takes a long time smoothing her clothes and even when they are smooth, perfectly smooth, smoother even than when she climbed over the fence, she still does not raise her head, and I see, even from here, where her highlights have grown out, and I begin to understand something about the high cost of upkeep.

They are gone and the chain link is still and I stretch my arms out and over my head, back and forth, back and forth, a dirt angel for the next plane. I push my hands up to the sky and spread my fingers wide apart, look at the thin, red groove that runs across both palms, from below my pinky to above my thumb, it cracks open and oozes, and when I stand up, brush off, and lift my head, I am face-to-face with Horse.

The clouds are nice, the planes are good, but Horse is the reason I come to the field because, just like the Girl Scouts say, in the Horseback Riding section of the *Handbook*, "A horse not only takes you over hill and dale, but he has a real personality of his own." He is only one horse, but he and his personality have a ton of field, and only sometimes does he make his way this far, and only sometimes does he come close to the fence.

Horse moved in right after junior high started. I was sitting on the bit of wall at the end of the Calle near the cesspond the day two men came near it with posts and wires, and when I came back the next day the wires went farther than I'm allowed to go, but there was nothing on the other side of the wires for days and days, nothing for the wires to do, and when there finally was a reason for them to be there, things to separate, the thing to be kept on one side was a horse and the thing to be kept on the other was me. I was pretty excited about him but he wasn't that excited about me. I came every day and stood in front of him, but he would move away or, worse, turn around. I told him all I'd learned from the *Girl Scout Handbook*, how close I was to being eligible for the Horsewoman badge without being able to do the four starred activities that require the use of an actual horse, the mysteries I had memorized about implements for grooming, removing stones, and

Western versus English saddles, but Horse had nothing to say. So then I'd sit down and look at him and he'd stare right past me. He wouldn't even shiver or wiggle his ears, swish his tail. Until finally I was just done trying to catch his stupid brown eyes and hold their attention and I reached out and grabbed the bottom wire of the fence with both hands and shook it like I wanted to shake him, and that is the exact second when I found out that Horse lives inside an electric cage.

His owner must have learned enough about the Calle to protect his possession from the questionable types circling its streets, but not enough to know that fences won't keep the criminals out, because the only real difference a fence makes is that jumping one is a crime and worry about that fades faster than the shock from the fence itself. The only thing worse than feeling pain around here is not feeling anything at all, so if we decide that we want to get at his horse, to tease it or feed it or ride it, if we decide this horse is the thing to do, a few volts aren't going to stop us. But no one's interested in the animal or the fence, except for me. Horse doesn't cramp Marc and DeShawn's make-out and smoking sessions, he's not human enough to fight or fuck and not old enough to buy them beer. Still, he's all I want, straight out of the storybooks. My very own pony.

psalms

Looking out the kitchen window, up the Calle, two cars are headed in this direction, two chances it might be Mama. Mama driving means she clocked out and walked out, but Mama walking means she took the long route home, through all the Calle's bars, down all the Calle's drinks. I watch the cars and hold the edge of the countertop tight, but when I look at my hands where the metal edge of the counter rubs the red electric lines running across my palms, memories of my visits to Horse, I forget to pay attention to where the rubber meets the road and my two cars rev by. The Calle grows quiet and I take the plastic butter dish into the dining room, sit down by the phone.

"Is Jo there?" I rub butter across one palm. "Okay. Thanks." I dial again. "Is Jo there?" I butter the other palm. "Have you seen her today?" Phone down. Phone back up. Hang it up, pick it up, hang it up. Pound the cradle so the bell shakes. There's breadcrumbs on the phone and the nine button is sticking I'm pushing it so hard, but I put on my best I'm-a-normal-kid voice when the ringing stops. "Hi, it's Ror." The bartenders don't even wait for me to ask, sometimes they don't even wait for my name but interrupt me to say, "Haven't seen her," or sometimes there's a hopeful pause while they hold the phone up high and look around before they say, "You just missed her," and ain't that the truth.

starvation ridge

My mother is a hungry dog.

I will always be a hungry dog like my mama, unable to remember when my dish was full or if it might be full again. I keep one eye on the dish, the other on the hand that descends. My teeth ache to bite, hold hand to mouth and never wonder again.

crushed

I wash the butter off my hands and fill a pot with water. There's no one on the street but I smile out the window anyway, say, "Hello! And welcome to *Cooking with Rory*! Thank you for tuning in. You're lucky because today we're making my specialty—Top Ramen! You will need a small pot for boiling water, and of course, one package of Top Ramen! You may notice that the directions suggest two cups of water, but in my years of perfecting this recipe I've found that half a pot works best." I hold up the pot for my audience and then slam it on the bag of noodles, saying, "Remember to crush the fucking noodles before opening the package." The package splits open, noodles fly everywhere, and I turn on a burner while scanning my audience for signs of approaching cars, but instead of cars, it's Marc. He's riding his bike down the middle of the street. His shirt is tucked into the back pocket of his jeans and I can see the hair on his chest that wasn't there before, curling and wet. He turns into his driveway and rides through the gate without even a look at our kitchen window where I am now doing anything but pretending to have my own cooking show and waiting like a dog for my mama. I forget about the soup altogether.

"Hello! And welcome to *Dialing with Rory*! Thank you for tuning in!" I say, as I look through the phone book for a new number to memorize. Marc's last name is Simmons, and I punch his number through butter and breadcrumbs. I swear I can hear his phone ringing from over the fence, and when he answers I hold my breath through all of his hellos and only breathe again when the dial tone starts.

the first and the fifteenth

The movement from hand to mouth is at once isolated and distinct but also automatic, unvarying.

right use of your body

I'm climbing back over the chain link from my last trip to visit Horse, my last time to shake hands with his electric fence, when I get it. It. First I go for the *Girl Scout Handbook*. I don't remember seeing anything about the protocol for this event but I'm sure it's there. I check everywhere, under *M* and *P*, under "Abdomen, first aid for pain in," and "Cuts (*see also* Wounds)," and finally I run my finger down column after column of the index, past "Color Guard" and "Dues, annual national membership," "Hitching tie," "Mammal badge," and "Snakes." Nothing. The Girl Scouts offer no advice for my condition, no ceremony, no supplemental material available for purchase by sending one dollar through the mail. There should at least be a patch, teardrop-shaped, to be sewn discreetly to the inside of the uniform, a waning moon embroidered over a field of cotton, a danger sign on the side of a thready mountain road.

When I tell Mama, she smiles, but it's slow in coming and gone by the time she stops hugging me, a long one like we were saying good-bye and her question is like that too: "Do you have everything you need?" I half expect her to hand me a quarter and ask me to call when I get there, wherever it is she's sending me off to, but I obey the first of the unwritten rules of puberty and act as if I know what's needed and certainly have it. Satisfied, she sits down to toast my womanhood with one Coors after another until she's celebrated so long she's passed out under the haze of a *Soap* rerun. I go back to the *Handbook* and exhaust "Stains, removal of" before settling for "Uniforms, disposing of outgrown." My blood-stained blue jeans go in the bag hidden at the bottom of my closet, the bag with the torn ruffled skirt and my favorite rainbow T-shirt, and I let the door close on it all.

make your request

I am lighting a candle. The candle is for Saint Jude. Not the famous-famous Jude who sold his friend for silver, not Iscariot, but Thaddeus. Saint Jude Thaddeus is the guy in charge of hopeless causes, of which I am one, despite what my scores on the standardized tests say. Unlike the kindly teachers at Roscoe, Jude is savvy to the real tests that lie ahead, and to that end, he has quite a line of candles. You've probably seen his name in the *Penny Saver* on Wednesdays. Jude's famous in the quiet way of saints kept near the back, two lines for $14.99, but he's in the papers all the time because Saint Jude works his ass off answering prayers. Telling others about the help he's granted is all he wants by way of payback. It doesn't take placing an ad to do this, either, so long as the news gets shared. Payback could be anything. It could be this.

So I'm lighting this candle. And I'm saying these words. I'm opening the windows and I'm turning off the lights. I'm lighting a candle to Saint Jude, in the dark, in the night, so the bugs will come, because tonight, I'm inviting insects. The wick is lit, it's irresistible in the dark, and I'm letting in Mama's fears and my own, let them duke it out for a space nearest the flame, settle this old score once and for all and see who's left standing when morning comes. Saint Jude's prayer is backlit on the candle's label and its words dance in shadow through the windows, flicker into corners,

219

and race across walls, *Saint Jude* and *name of the traitor* and *desperate cases* and *pray for me who am so miserable* and *implore* and *consolation* and then there's a space for the supplicants, of which I am one, to state the exact nature of the trouble:

_____

(make your request here)

free love

Having a one-time hippie for a mom means no church on Sundays, but there's other stuff to worship. The bookshelf is full and I read through *I'm OK—You're OK* and learn that no one promised me a rose garden. I read *This Is Women's Work* and learn never to eat the yellow wallpaper. I read Kerouac and many books by the Prophet and learn that all work is empty except when there is love, but even Gibran's compassion can't fill the emptiness in Mama's checkbook, so it's off to work she goes, which used to mean I'd be off to Carol's, where the bookshelves were empty of books but full of dusty snow globes and greasy parts catalogues, and used to mean I'd be off to Grandma's, where the baskets were full of skeins of yarn, crochet hooks, and poker chips, and now it means I'm stuck here with all these books I've already read. Having a one-time hippie for a mom means that she treats me like a grown-up, I can cuss, and I can have birth control as soon as I ask. And it means I can ask for other things too, like to leave, like my brothers did. And it means that she'd probably let me go.

proficiency badge: puberty

 Symbol: *The Girl Scout salute, three fingers extended, the thumb holding down the little finger*

To earn this badge do five of these activities, the three starred are required.

1. Act as if you know more about the following things than you do: sanitary pads, parked cars, birth control, love.

★2. Forget to change your pad long enough to allow a silver-dollar-sized spot of blood to leak through to the seat of your pants. Intermediate: Have a boy notice the spot before you do. Advanced: Have the boy who notices it be the one you secretly have a crush on (or his best friend).

3. Know at least five euphemisms for menstruation, including: the curse, falling off the roof, and having Aunt Flo pay a visit.

★4. Gain a new respect for bleach. Intermediate: Gain a new respect for black underwear. Advanced: Consider the difference between kid underwear and sexy ones. Make sure that at least one of your sexy pairs features a heart-shaped patch. If a heart-shaped patch cannot be found, rhinestones or a cherry appliqué may be substituted.

5. Know which shelf holds the Judy Blume books at your school library. Be able to tell from across the room whether or not they are checked out. Intermediate: Know their Dewey Decimal numbers by heart. Advanced: Keep a list of the most enlightening scenes on the girls' bathroom wall.

6. Sleep with a bra on every night in fear of your boobs dropping should you forget. Intermediate: Don't wear a bra in the daytime. Advanced: Forget bras and wear the *Here Comes Trouble* T-shirt you got for your eighth birthday. Act offended if anyone stares at the new shape of the word *Trouble*. Wear the shirt until your mother asks what smells.

★7. Discover that the merest mention of menstrual pain causes your P.E. teacher's eyes to glaze over. Understand that she is inept at keeping track of dates and will not remember when your last period was. Use this understanding to sit on the bleachers until finals.

8. Sneak your mother's makeup to cover your acne. Intermediate: Also sneak her mascara. Advanced: Don't sneak any of it because, fuck them, if they want to stare at your tits they can stare at your zits, too.

make a wish

                              HENDRIX, Johanna #310,788
MEDICAL HISTORY AND PHYSICAL EXAMINATION

There is a family history of tuberculosis. The
mother was found to have a small spot in her
lung but apparently no active tuberculosis. She
was counseled in May 1971 at the Mental Health
Service but she doesn't feel that it benefited
her much. She feels, in general, she is treating
the children much better but that maybe this is
"too late." She is currently four months
pregnant and does not intend to marry this
baby's father.

                                        V. White:wr

                                        11-27-72

"This is the year you don't get pregnant," Mama says, and even
though there are presents wrapped on the table, I know this wish is
her real gift to me, a chance at control, a chance at my own life. I
was going to make a wish of my own, but hers burns so hot and
bright over my fifteen candles that all I can do is blow them out,
this wish she didn't make for herself over her own fifteenth birth-

224

day cake, or made but couldn't keep. Maybe even made again the year she became pregnant with me, somehow deciding to hold on to me and leave behind the man who was my father.

What she'll leave. What will be mine. The list of things: furniture, papers, wedding ring. Mama can see her death coming early, the smoke rising over the ridge, the scar of TB on her lungs. Only poets, libertines, and poor people get TB, and the pure force of Mama's birthday wish, the balls it takes to make a wish for someone else, right out loud in front of them, makes me think she might have some poetry in her soul after all. My brothers can have the other stuff she's so anxious to leave behind. This is all I want to inherit.

like a diamond in the sky

A pair of headlights appears at the entrance to the Calle and there is a woman on the street, but she cannot be my mama, even though she is tall and long-legged, even though she follows the route that leads to our house, the one that leads to me. Tonight this stranger blinks and steadies herself against the neons that shimmy and blur, blend against a pair of headlights twinkle-twinkling so far she barely wonders what they are, headlights that glitter a promise just beyond the Hardware Store.

The headlights grow larger and still with their own story to tell, their own anger and appetite. The woman walking Mama's route has one more lane to go. The white lines glow brighter before her. She blinks down at them. These lines do not jumble up or play games. Their message is clear. She turns her head sharply in the direction of the light, grown too close too fast, wailing and white. She glares at the brightness and intimacy, opens her mouth. And then she flies.

There is screeching and the smell of burning rubber.

And Mama, because it is my mama, if it was a stranger it wouldn't feel like this, like my own bones breaking, like my own good-bye I'm saying, comes down twenty feet away from the skid marks left by Stu Holman's pickup truck on the pavement of the busiest curve on the Calle. Inside the cab, Stu's hand slides against metal and plastic. Inside the cab, Stu cannot find the door handle, doesn't understand how to work the lock.

The customers who appear in the windows and screen door of the Truck Stop pour onto the Calle like sticky fluid and watch Stu as he collapses on the bug-splattered grill of his truck, trying to breathe in the muggy air. Mosquitoes, moth wings, stick on the back of his jacket. Sounds begin to lap against the thickness in the air like a tide coming in, the sounds of quarreling, sobbing, the sound of beer glass shattering on asphalt, the sound of sirens.

girlchild

help with fractions

If a pickup truck with ½ tank of gas driven by a man 0.02 under the legal limit enters the Calle at ¼ to last call while Mama drinks at the Truck Stop at a constant rate of speed until she's reached ½ cocked and her money ½ spent, how long will it take for the news to reach me, sleeping, the television on?
(Show all of your work.)

A) *The dad has to sit 5 feet from the fulcrum.*
B) *Working together they can complete the job in 2.4 minutes.*
C) *The basket contains 7 yellow onions.*
D) *It will take 2⅓ candles to light her way home.*

desolation angels

I'm sleeping when there is a knock on the door. It's early, before five, and dark, but I turn off the TV and slide the door open because I can see by the pink rising over the hill beyond my window that it's my brothers waiting outside. All of them. Hendrix. Hendrix. Hendrix. Hendrix.

I'm too young to know that this early, unexpected visit means Mama's employee file has been opened and the entries under Who to Contact in Case of an Emergency have been read, to know there was a fight about who would ride in the ambulance and who would make the call. For once, I'm too young to see what's coming and there's no getting out of the way. My brothers are hours from where they live in the bright-lights-big-city that hardly casts a shadow on the Calle and so neither do they. One sentence later and it's too late to not know why their rush, the breakneck speed to tell me the news themselves before I hear the eleven o'clock version on the Calle. One sentence later and it's too late to be too young again.

It's Ronnie who says it first, "Mama was in an accident, she was hit by a truck," and my own scream surprises me. I don't know that's my voice filling the room until I feel Ronnie's arms wrapping around me, holding me, and the noise doesn't stop even after Bob and Gene and Winston move in close. We hold each other on Mama's patchwork carpet, grip a hand or a shoulder, but I scream for all of us because there are no other sounds.

clipped

Johanna Ruth Hendrix, 46, died Monday at Saint Mary's Regional Medical Center.

A native of Santa Cruz, Calif., she was born July 31, 1943, and had been a Reno resident for the past 11 years.

Mrs. Hendrix worked in the food service industry.

Surviving are her daughter, R.D. Hendrix, age 15; son, son, son, and son Hendrix, ages 24 to 30; father, John Gunthum, whereabouts unknown; mother, Shirley Crumb; and leagues of empty barstools and even emptier beer glasses.

Cremation will be at the Masonic Memorial Gardens Crematory, under direction of the Alan Sparks Memorial Cremation Society.

A memorial is being established with the Sun Valley Lions Club, P.O. Box 20068, Sun Valley 89431. A service is scheduled for 11 a.m. Saturday at the Truck Stop.

Bring casserole.

and this too shall pass

My brothers sit on lawn chairs and I park myself on the gravel in front of them, hide myself in the stubble of their five o'clock shadows and feel like the newest fifth wheel on the Calle, a whisper of my own capital *H*. We went to Hobee's for breakfast, but they should have saved their money because we didn't make a dent in the buffet. And now we're sitting together in front of the Nobility trying to figure out what to do next. The gravel pokes my ass as I watch my four brothers, grown men already getting ready to say good-bye to their twenties, consider how to help me get my feet on the ground, a little sister they hardly know. Each has a wife, common law or otherwise, and already too many mouths to feed to offer to take me. I wouldn't go with them anyway and maybe they know that, remember it from having made a choice like this themselves once and at a similar age, and that is why we talk around it. No one suggests my living with Grandma either. We all know that her Social Security check provides just enough to keep her poor without taking me on, even including what the Social Security office might see fit to provide by way of what they do not hesitate to call Surviving Child Benefits. I could go to Grandma's and be her final burden. She wouldn't complain but she knows, and we know, the time has come for me to get on with growing up. I don't need my brothers and Grandma doesn't need me. It's the Calle or the highway, and so the first adult understanding between us begins with this: I'll take care of myself. All

that remains is to figure out how to guarantee a minimum of inter-
ference on the part of the County. And how to say good-bye to
Mama.

The first part is easy; we've been working around the County
our whole lives. It won't even take having the County look the
other way, if we don't ask them for anything, looking the other way
is what they'll do, and as soon as I'm sixteen, I'll emancipate myself, which is County talk for become an adult on paper.

The second part is something new and takes a lot of cigarettes,
smoked to the quick, to even begin to figure out. I watch them
smoke and talk it out, talk her out, our late, great mama, figure out
what our two versions of her have in common and what they
don't.

"I never really got in trouble for anything," I say, and Gene says
he did once, really caught it, "For smoking pot outside the house,"
and Bob says, "For cussing around strangers." The pot was before
my time, when Mama was still kid enough to rock her shelves with
Kerouac without needing to know just why she should. When she
was still kid enough to send her own kids off to school with hair so
long they got beat for it. Hendrix. Hendrix. Hendrix. Hendrix.
The 4 H Club. My brothers grew up with too much beat and not
enough rhythm in a house, an actual house, full of Buddhas and
Nag Champa, prayer flags and peace signs. But our house, Mama's
and mine, has wheels and is kept so clean it's always ready to roll,
and except for the fading mint of Benson & Hedges the air is
clear, and except for a beaded sign that decorates the top of our
corkboard, the colors of its purple, gold, and black beads blending
with the darkening shades of the electric bills pinned below, the
sign that says AND THIS TOO SHALL PASS AWAY, nothing of that
old house, nothing of that old Mama remains. The sign is right;
when Mama came to Reno she left that life behind. If it weren't for
these few relics that make the Nobility different from the other
trailers in our row, it would feel almost like my brothers and I

didn't have the same mother at all except for, as the 4-H Club and I are discovering, her lenience, her lack of chores and penalties, and her fear. They remember her being afraid and not knowing of what, but I'm the only one who still feels her demands, her grip on my shoulders, her eyes brown and sharp as bottle glass, her voice telling me what she never told her boy children, saved instead for a girlchild.

"Smoke follows beauty," she liked to say, and their smoke burns through Mama's life, climbs and ducks through her ups and downs, and it's a pattern I recognize, so it must be our same mama after all, theirs and mine, share and share alike, but just when I think we've got her agreed on, the smoke turns quick, gathers, darkens, and folds itself into the shape of a man. Winston is making a list of who we need to call, and Grandma is calling Mama's sisters from her trailer in California, and I say, "What about Grandpa Gun?" but once the name is said it blows back against the 4-H Club like thunder clapping, close enough to make me shiver, and numbers begin to rise automatically in my head. It's Mama's voice teaching, telling me to "count the number of seconds between the thunder and the lightning, that's how close the danger is, girlchild."

Thunderclaps, and I stop counting, and say a sound that is equal to the number of seconds since the light flashed jagged, since Grandpa appeared here in front of the Nobility double-wide where he's never been allowed. The number is supposed to be equal to the number of miles away we are from the approaching storm, but I can tell from my brothers' faces that we're already in it and before I can stop myself, the next sounds I make slant up at the end, curl themselves into questions, and the smoke that has taken Grandpa's shape swallows my questions back down into my still-open mouth, and settles itself across my lungs like the dark bands of asphalt that bind the Calle, and my brothers begin their talk about Gun, the myths and hazy truths, and the two versions of him there are too.

Ronnie says that Grandpa thought dress-up time was shoot-out time, but Gene throws in, for no reason at all that I can see, "Mama never was deaf in one ear, just pretending. He never touched us." It's all mixed-up, top and bottom, these stories of Grandpa and his daughters, what he did and didn't do: pale skin during a moment of touch, four little girls surviving a shotgun shack, so like Mama's little boys surviving the cabin on the ridge the night she tried to take them all down. I wonder how many of her words, screamed at air, were for him. How many of her warnings about pretty dresses and bathing suit string were said too strong to me because they were too late for her. And then it's enough. Enough to start a sweat creeping across my back, to unspool the memory of seeing Grandpa once in real life, flesh and blood not smoke and mirrors, his pick-up truck to pick me up after school. He said Grandma was "off somewheres," that Mama needed him to get me. And he said I should call him Grandpa, his fingers on the steering wheel red from cold, calluses rising sharp and clear, the Braille of the working class. I could read his age from his hands, I could guess his trade, but his sins went silent as fingerprints and the lights on the Calle start to flicker and the insects begin their crawl, under the skin, trying to find a way out, they trail up my arms, push the hairs to stand at attention.

Grandpa Gunthum says he's taking me to Kmart to buy me any doll I want, "No matter what anybody has to say about it," and then, "up to ten dollars." I'm standing in the toy aisle facing one way and the other, feeling stared at by this strange Grandpa and by the dolls, lined up for the taking. I'm wondering what it might have took for Grandma to send him to pick me up from school in her place, and feeling pressure in my thighs from not knowing how to pick a new doll or if I should pick one at all, and I twist my foot around my ankle and begin examining the patch on my pocket.

Grandpa wants to know why I'm taking so long, and I say that if I could hold the money myself it would help me decide, so he hands the bills over, and then I pick a doll quick and pay the checkout lady myself, trying to make sure Grandpa doesn't think just because he bought me a doll it makes me his Holly Hobbie.

There were lots of things Mama never learned how to do and too many things she shouldn't have had to learn, her future spun early like a knife-thrower's wheel, the making and unmaking of a rotten-mouthed girl, the histories of a feebleminded daughter. Mama couldn't see anything except what happened to her, her story spelled out over and over again. And I can't see what happens in the shadows created by the Hardware Man, but those shadows mark that something was lost, and that's how I know that Grandpa didn't cast his shadow on me, because I can remember that day. But Mama couldn't have believed it, and I finally understand why, why she couldn't think her father might hold tighter to regret than he ever held her and would only try to push his way back into our lives for an afternoon in order to prove to himself that he could. For all my yelling against history, for all the spelling bee chances I've lost and the chances I might have left, when my mama's life was decided, mine was too, at least in her eyes. She didn't like coming home then and she won't be coming home now, but at least I know why. All this time she thought that she hadn't saved me the way she hadn't been saved, but there's more than one way to save a kid, and maybe my brothers just did it, by telling me about Grandpa Gun and the real reason Mama didn't like coming home at night.

My brothers survived her craziest years in one piece and never got close enough to risk body or soul again. But you have to come home when someone dies, because blood is thicker than tar and all the scrubbing in the world won't stop your good and bad blood flowing forever together through your veins, meeting in a rush at corners, gathering force, and washing you back up on the Calle. Now they've done their duty by seeing if they're needed, and I've done my duty by telling them they're not. We've made our plans, for my survival, for my new life on the Calle. We've got a pack of lies to deal to the County, should they ever come knocking. The good brothers are rowing back home to the lives they somehow figured out how to make once the Ridge was behind them, and I hug them good-bye and stand under the awning to watch their taillights fade.

paper dolls

It's not like I haven't ever cracked the hope chest's lid before, but I only looked at the letters bundled on the top, then closed it quick again. I never moved anything around, never so much as pulled a ribbon on those stacks. Mama's superstitions were as hereditary as anything else, and I was afraid of upsetting the balance she'd arranged with old man Death. I never stepped on cracks, either, but this is mine now and the lid sounds different when I open it, quieter, like it knows I'm not sneaking this time. It's warped from the plant Mama kept on it, and I lean its curve against the wall and start taking out papers. And the first answer to my questions about "What's in the hope chest?" about "What's so important?" is: a lot. A body can sure hold on to a lot of paper in a lifetime, even a short one, and when that body's gone, not many of those papers make sense.

Here are a few things of Mama's: every assignment I ever brought home, even from kindergarten, bundles of letters from Grandma to her, every single card my brothers ever sent, even if all they wrote on it themselves was their name, was a first initial. Nothing is that surprising, though, until I find a set of pictures almost in full color. They're of a swimming pool and trees. And my brothers. Hendrix. Hendrix. Hendrix. Hendrix. Mama isn't in any of them, but it's easy to imagine her standing worried by that water, afraid for her boys. They must have visited a place with a pool, they're splashing around in it, their briefs all the same, stripes running horizontally across. They look happy, the flash doesn't scare them at all, and I wonder if that's why Mama kept these pictures, particularly these. To remind herself that whatever else she didn't do, she made sure all of her children knew how to survive in elements she would never master.

And there's a picture of me that Mama took. I'm wearing the suit I wore to the lake that summer, a two-piece the color of wine lipstick, shimmery and dark, light purple lines curling over the tops of my not-yet breasts, swinging up in waves around the bottoms. I can tell from the look on my face that I'm impatient to get away from the camera and into the lake that rolls out behind me.

There are black-and-white photos too. Mama and her sisters wearing matching dresses like the Girl Scouts of Other Nations in the illustrated section of the *Girl Scout Handbook*. They stand in perfectly graduated height and I'm dizzy when I look into their eyes, eyes about the same age as mine. It's like the photos become a pop-up book, their helplessness cut from the paper and scored, they take shape on my lap and I feel Mama's hands squeezing, her eyes bright and begging, but I don't know what she wants anymore or who she's asking.

Underneath the pictures there is a thick bunch of legal-sized papers, curled up on the end from so many years in the hope chest, from all the miles it's traveled in our immobile mobile home. There is a small note on top addressed to Johanna Ruth Hendrix c/o The Santa Cruz Legal Aid Society, and it tells her, "The County of Santa Cruz protests the release of this information," and the information whose release is being protested is my mama's, my family's, my own. The reports, written by V. White and the State of California, are linear and sure, they're positive about times and places, make no bones about guilt or truth, and they begin like this:

CHRONOLOGICAL RECORD

HENDRIX, Johanna Ruth
116 Holway Drive
Santa Cruz, California

funeral etiquette

When a Calle resident passes on, it is customary to not know what to do, say, or where to look. The very phrase "passes on" can be confusing as it implies a forward motion hitherto unfamiliar on Calle streets. This confusion is natural, and for Calle residents who aren't directly affected by the death, meeting those in mourning for the departed soul is best avoided. However, if the waning supply of frozen meals necessitates leaving the house, for example, or one drink is in order after the day you've had, the following guidelines will assist in handling most encounters with a minimum of discomfort.

A primary goal during any occasion for mourning taking place on the Calle is to have one's actions be as inoffensive as possible. The bolder acquaintances of the deceased will make a phone call or perhaps deliver a store-bought card. The less bold will attempt sympathetic shapes with smoke rings from the safety of their kitchen table and say nothing. Mass cards or other devotional objects do not come into play here except for the usual found at every kitchen table on the Calle: cut decks brought home from the casinos, the machined slit at the top alerting handlers that this deck is too worn for the tables and gamblers whose soft hands learn the nuances of a worn card faster than the shape of a woman's curves. During such times, these cards are shuffled more thoughtfully than usual, the dealer often needing to be reminded to deal, of the game still being played by the living.

In lieu of the usual mementos, then, souvenirs in the form of paperwork are distributed directly to those suffering most. Early visitors will assist the bereaved, especially if she is underage, with application forms for social security (SSDI) and surviving child benefits (Form 410-414), with discussions of emancipation if deemed necessary, and with the kind of grief that turns one into an adult overnight (see Form 831b, use black ink only).

If you'd like to contribute something to the memorial, flowers say all you can't and shouldn't. Be they gladiolas, wisteria, or toilet paper, a floral arrangement is simple and meaningful, a comfort to the mourner who will miss her mother's sure hand in the garden. Your florist or bartender can guide you in selecting something appropriate.

Attire in this circumstance should be considerately chosen. The cleanest shirt with the most buttons still attached for men and longer skirts, to the knee if possible, for women. Floral patterns should be avoided, and uniforms of any sort are frowned upon.

Once at the actual funeral, if you are unfamiliar with the customs of the family in mourning, follow the lead of others. This will usually take you to the ice chest wherein you will find ice-cold beverages. The bottle opener will be attached to a string on one of the ice chest's handles. After you've had some refreshment, pay your respects to the person who has died by having a bit more. If you are worried about what to say or what not to say to those surviving, some examples of phrases better avoided are "She was a piece of ass" and "Live by the bottle, die by the bottle."

Specific foods are prepared in mourning situations, often the same ones consumed in front of the television during car races, the interminable circles of the cars mimicking the circles of the Calle as well as the circles of life and death. After filling your plate with potato salad and beans it is appropriate to become completely smashed, putting your arms around strangers and sobbing heartbreak over the deceased. Your very presence will thus add meaning to the occasion, whether you eventually pass out or not.

The question about whether children should be present at the memorial is best answered with other common questions asked at this time, such as: Where else would they go? and, Who would watch them? Most important, however, is the question: Where else could they acquire the necessary tools for coping with adulthood's losses without this atmosphere to provide the appropriate conditions? Funerals are usually where Calle pubescents have their first drinks, as the adults around them realize that life is indeed too short and distribute the alcohol themselves.

Many Calle teens have their first sexual experiences during funerals and memorials. There is no doubt that usually subdued teenagers find these experiences an incredibly meaningful way to express their grief. It is important, however, to advise children, teens, and those who just act like them, to be on their best behavior. For example, one should never slip behind the Porta-John brought for the day's function and kiss her neighbor, who wears his father's leather jacket and reeks of cologne, should never kiss him right on the mouth and find that his lips are bigger than they look, that his tongue is cold, and that, even though his dad's jacket almost fits him now and despite all the practice he's had in the field behind their two houses, much of which she's witnessed, he doesn't kiss like a man at all.

If a mourner did suffer this slip in decorum, she would surely say something after the kiss and not run around to the front of the Porta-John and turn the handle, would never hide inside, climbing on the lid of the toilet to watch through the vent as the boy, and boy he is, returns to his seat and high-fives his friend. The high-fives betray his belief that he's caused feelings to flower in her, which will alleviate the pain of this new crushing reality, instead of the ones he's actually made bloom, cheap and tough as funeral carnations: nausea and instant regret.

For further details on how to behave under these sorrowful circumstances, refer to more comprehensive works, such as those by Emily Post or the Manners section of the *Girl Scout Handbook*.

caution: children

Pigeon left a casserole on the porch. It's left over from the Lions Club picnic held yesterday in Mama's honor. They pushed the tables together behind the Truck Stop, stacked them high with pies and wieners and potato salad, and threw the back door open wide so the jukebox could save us from talking. I managed to stay even after I kissed Marc behind the Porta-John, but the thought of food only reminded me of his disgusting tongue, so when "Blue Eyes Crying in the Rain" came on, I snuck in the back door and out the front and headed unseen for home. At least that's what I thought, but Pigeon must have noticed and that's why she brought the casserole. Tuna, with peas. I didn't answer the door but I watched her through a corner of the curtain, knocking and calling and then setting down the dish, tightening the tinfoil around its edges.

I don't eat it even though I like to look at it, and there's no other food in the Nobility that's still good, though I can't bring myself to throw away the sliced cheese turning to liquid in the wrapper, the milk turning solid in the carton. I'm pretty sure I'm not hungry, that I can't get hungry, that I've forgotten how, and I'm happy like that until a melancholy music makes me remember. The Four Humors Ice-Cream Truck is coming slowly down the Calle. Not playing its usual ragtime ditty, the echo of a sweet sugar high, but instead, the saddest song that ever made its never-ending way through scratchy speakers and across front yards. The most forlorn music ever to entice children from Big Wheels and jump ropes comes rippling down the Calle, and before I know I've decided, I'm reaching into the tip jar, stepping to the door, down the porch, sliding in between parked cars to stand on the Calle and be noticed by the Ice Cream Man.

As he climbs from the driver's seat to the window in the back, the truck lurches under his weight. I can smell his sweat before I see his face. His onion odor mixes with the sweet sugar of pixie sticks and licorice that hang down in a tangle of Christmas lights from the window's top and sides. The twinkling lights rinse the Ice Cream Man's face in alternating shades of red and pink and green.

He does not speak, but inclines his head to the side to indicate the fading menu and then looks down at the pavement so pointedly that I follow his eyes and find my order there at my feet, in the way the skid marks almost curl into letters, reminding me. "Two drumsticks," I say. Mama's favorite.

He takes the money with one hand, and with the other turns a switch on a lamp whose bare lightbulb reveals cardboard boxes and cases of soda stacked to the ceiling. He holds first one bill and then the other up to the bulb, examines each side carefully, then sets them on a six-pack of root beer and opens the freezer in front of him with its stickers of spiral-eyed, upside-down children enjoying giant popsicles in the shapes of rocket ships and atom bombs. They stand on their heads, frown at their ice creams. The dry sound of ice scraping against ice reaches me with the shuffling of frozen cardboard and rasp of the Ice Cream Man's breathing. His voice comes around the freezer's lid, more melancholy than the music that still fills the air. "Don't go," he says. "I have it right here."

The spiral-eyed children fall away as the Ice Cream Man pushes two drumsticks through the canopy of candy and lights. His face shines red and green, is so slick I can't tell the difference between sweat and tears.

I open up one drumstick as I walk up the Calle. Flowers, candles, mementos are accumulating on the shoulder, washing up from the road, from the river of people that have come by to pay their respects. I kneel down beside a bouquet of toilet paper roses decorated with drops of dew-like glue, the saints whose faces glow from Save-Rite-bought candles, San Gerardo Maiella, San Martín de Porres, San Simón, Niño Jesús, and Saint Jude. Other candles with no visible saints flicker or have died. Purple and white and yellow wax puddle the asphalt. There is a picture of "Johanna," so the writing on the label says, preflight. It is a picture of a picture, fuzzy, and too small in the round frame. I finish my drumstick, and then I leave the unopened one to melt between a rosary and a wooden truck, a dirty length of yarn tied through its front bumper.

gifted

Grandma's sent my sixteenth birthday gift from her Space 2 on Taylor Street in Portola, California, far from casinos and the desert wind. It arrives wrapped in a shoebox, furniture for a doll's room made from crochet and scrap: shag rug, bureau with embroidered gold handle, bed with mattress, quilt and pillow, fireplace with twig and paper to burn, a bent paperclip as its grate, and a hope chest whose lid hinges back to reveal the links of stones, small as beans before they sprout, their chain broken here and here, together in a row as long as ten, apart alone as one. And with them, her instructions, to protect them, to join them, as if the people of a family could be held together with gold plate and hot glue. And just below that, one more tear from Grandma's felt-tip on onionskin, *a few more make believes for one of your shelves*. The furniture is for the little girl I'm not anymore, the one Grandma and I are both saying good-bye to. The stones are for the adult that even the State is starting to recognize, the woman I've become, and what Grandma thinks that woman might do.

Grandma swears that one day a Hendrix will shine bright enough to light her world, or a corner of it, or at least her table where she sits and drinks her beer with ice and listens to talk radio deep into the night, her television gone, sold to buy drugs for one of her children, food for one of her grandchildren. Always stolen from, always replacing, always forgiving, always believing, that sums up Grandma Shirley Rose and this is her summing up of me. Even

250

before the Briefcase Men started showing up at Roscoe Elementary, before my name appeared in the *Gazette*, Grandma had these words to say, quietly, over coffee and oatmeal, over RC and bologna sandwiches, "Someone's got to make it and it has to be you," her sweet, sick Grandma smell mixing with the smoke of her cigarettes, the cold breeze from the Calle, and the sage-and-sandpaper sound of her voice, pushing me to do it, to take my chance, to make belief.

dream

The *Girl Scout Handbook* has a section on Finding Your Way When Lost and I just about know it by heart. The number one most important thing for a Scout to do is to stay where the rest of her party last saw her. I'm waiting at the wall down by the landfill I call a pond because the wall's the oldest thing around and there isn't much of it left. It's only a few feet long and only about that high, but the stones don't budge, and for all the spray paint, the grass keeps growing up around it. I don't know what the wall used to do before we got here, but I'm using it for waiting, I'm using it for not panicking, and, like the *Handbook* says, most important, I'm using it for not wearing myself out by aimless wandering.

I'm waiting for Grandma. We are going to the greenhouse. I can't explain the presence of the greenhouse, rusted and nearly roofless. It slants at the far edge of the pond, the door forever swung open. The greenhouse is the only place on the Calle that has a memory of the possibilities for careful nurturing that lie even within an aluminum frame, even in a portable home, the delicacy in the hothouse promise. This one had been empty for years, I think, until Grandma arrived, which she does most nights, even though, no matter how hard I look, I've never seen Mama in a dream or anyplace else.

We go inside the greenhouse and Grandma points above our heads. At first all I see are slices of night sky showing through the

252

ribs that are all that is left of the roof. But Grandma is patient, and so am I, and I begin to make out that there are thin whorls of metal separating us from the slants of starlight. Chicken wire has been rolled from one side of the building to the other just above us, leaving a few feet between itself and the arched frame of the roof. The wire's coils and circles are coated with a fine layer of rust. I know it's rust because I touch it when Grandma tells me to, because I do what Grandma tells me to, I bring some of it down to crumble between my fingers, burning orange and rough, and I feel something else there. Roots. The tiniest plants have somehow twisted their roots round the coils of chicken wire, have taken root in the air. They brace themselves against the thin wire, draw nourishment from the metal, and grow straight toward the sky as if soil were only a myth.

pretty theft

I never met V. White outside the pages of Mama's welfare file and was barely getting to know her, anyway, when one afternoon, not too long after my brothers and I had our caucus, a man from the County came down to the Calle, parked his sedan on the gravel, and though it was broad daylight, checked his car's alarm twice before knocking at my door. V. White may be long gone, but the County lives on, and I tell the new guy the story we'll use until my emancipation is finalized. I tell it just the way my brothers and I rehearsed: my third-oldest brother, Ronald Joseph, is my legal guardian and has moved to the Calle permanently until I finish school, but he isn't home just now.

The Worker is as unmoved as the embroidered horse running in place across the left pocket of his shirt. He asks if he might use the bathroom before he leaves, to which I say that he might, though I know that this errand has less to do with relieving himself and more to do with relieving his curiosity. His real reason for venturing out to the Calle is to check the Nobility for signs of my brother's life and while none of my bros are actually coming to stay, we've covered our bases. A can of shaving cream sits rusting on the bathroom counter for just such an emergency, and while the Worker takes his tour, I sit on the couch and find myself face-to-face with my own reflection in the shiny gold locks of his briefcase. And that's when I do something the elder Hendrixes and I haven't rehearsed. I reach out my finger, just one finger, and push. And the

254

shiny gold locks go SMACK! down the hallway, the sound flattening up against the closed bathroom door.

The sweat from my fingers clouds the metal as I lift back the lid, and there, in between a yellow legal pad and the latest edition of *Barely Legal*, is an accordion file, and inside it, filed under *H* for Hendrix, under *T* for Trash, and under *L* for Living on the County, is a slick set of papers that are surprisingly familiar, copied from carbon, with V. White's and Mama's names and a case number running across the top of each one. And I develop a quick filing system of my own. I file those papers fast under *S* for Sofa, *C* for Cushion, and *M* for Mine, and then I close the briefcase up, quiet as you please. And I know this will stay quiet too, because if the Worker even suspects I'm the one who took the file, he'll know I've seen his magazine and won't want his boss to learn just how those unaccounted-for minutes of the County's time are spent. When the Worker comes back into the living room he finds his briefcase right where he left it and he looks me up and down slowly and says, "You're still a sophomore, aren't you, Rory Dawn? Just turned sixteen?"

I nod yes, in my most *Barely Legal* of fashions, trying to prepare myself for what's coming next, but it isn't the warning about minors living without supervision that I feared. The Worker may be coming on to me but he's not actually onto me. He doesn't suspect anything. His question, predictable and ridiculous, proves it. "It's never too early," he says, and he pauses as he reaches down for his briefcase, his eyes on my bare feet, "It's never too early to start thinking about the future. What are your plans after graduation?"

I suck my teeth, feeling my chipped front tooth, the jagged edge that's never been a priority to fix, and I give the Worker, like all the Briefcase Men who've come before him, the answer he's looking for. "I was thinking about vocational school," I say, remembering the counselor's recommendation to Mama from her welfare file, the copy whose twin I just stole back from him. My feet itch from his staring and I rub them on the carpet, trying to figure out what he's waiting for, and then I've got it. "I mean, if my grades are good enough."

It's the right answer, all right. The relief shows on his face. Secure that his job will be an easy one, that *Hendrix, R.D.*, can fall safely off his radar screen, he asks for Ronnie to give him a call, and then he leaves. I watch him take the turn off the gravel onto the cement, and then I take the stack of papers out from beneath the couch cushion and put them in the hope chest where all the other ideas of Mama's worth have washed up. If the Worker, with his suspicions and his habits, with his locks and his logos, thinks for a minute that his documents are any kind of testament, if he thinks he can read me just because he can read these, well, as Grandma would say, "He's got another think coming."

sophomore attempt

Stephanie Harris is pregnant, her once-proud upper-middle-class white collar has turned a deep crimson blush from shame, and I wonder what wish her Mama made over her fifteenth-birthday cake. Boys still go to Jupiter to get more stupider, but girls work at bars to get their candy bars, at least I do. During the day I have to go to school, though, or Pigeon says she'll eighty-six me herself.

I go to shop class and hear the whispers that I'm only taking it to see Marc, but really it's because everything else seems pointless. Cars, at least, can get you somewhere. There's no way to make sense of Mr. Lane's drafting class after Mama's accident, no way to draw angles and arcs. When the standardized tests come, I color my bubbles in a zigzag pattern, design a crooked heart, and still get a C. At breaks I sit alone in the quad and eat licorice from the vending machine, and after a month, all I've learned is my locker combination and that as soon as I can figure out how, I'm outta here.

ownself

Pigeon lets me hang out at the Truck Stop after school, but only if I bring my homework along. I wash glasses by the trayload and inventory the empty Coors and Olympia kegs that wait in the backyard to be picked up by the delivery man, and I count the unopened bottles of bottom-shelf whiskey and gin that wait in the stockroom to be drunk up by the regulars. I broke four glasses so far, but Pigeon says that my doing the inventory makes up for it, because, she says, and it's a lie, I'm the mathematical genius and she's got no head for numbers. The rest of the time I sit around and "get my studying in." I spread it out and lay down a pencil, but there's no point in any of it except for *The Divine Comedy*, assigned by our new English teacher whose first year at Roscoe hasn't beaten the life out of her yet. At least Dante's circles of damnation are a good match for the curves of the Calle that I follow on my way from school to the Truck Stop every afternoon.

I'd rather just sit and watch Pigeon do her work, watch the regulars take their seats like an assembly line shift, watch the night pull its own barstool right up to the edge of the screen door. I sit around at the table by the jukebox that still only plays country, underneath the cardboard signs and their one prayer, repeated to the infinite, HOGS AND CALVES FOR SELL. And I tell the new guys, when they ask if I'd like a drink knowing I can't be old enough, when they ask if I'd like a drink hoping I can't be old enough, that the only thing getting felt around here is the pool table.

And if I promise I'll finish my homework, and if no one's in but Dennis and the Ice Cream Man, Pigeon lets me go behind the bar and practice mixing drinks. My screwdriver is coming along but Pigeon says my martini "deserves a warning sign," and it's all a waste of cheap liquor, anyway, because no one around here orders anything but shots and chasers. Still, she lets me keep trying. She takes one sip of each and throws the rest away, and there's something so pretty about the sound of ice cubes ringing against a metal sink, about the way that Pigeon says, "Better try again tomorrow," that makes me feel like I will.

local dive

The Calle is silent except for the sound of my bare feet on the steps. The slap of skin on cement. The television shadows are dying down to static, preparing for rebirth in the plumage of the rainbow test pattern whose sudden brightness will wake sleepers to the loss of another night, the empty hours to go before morning.

I walk to the edge of the pond and stare at the crepe paper and candy wrappers, the waste still left from the last Revival Night that floats on its surface. The aluminum of beer cans star in the sand and the water is ink. There are words at its bottom, answers down there, and the spelling is shaky at best.

On the other side of the pond comes another girl, she has no clothes and her hands move quickly over herself, to hide or hurt, it seems the same. The motion is frantic, as if she's caught in a wind. Sometimes she uses her hands to cover her body. Sometimes she uses them to cover her mouth. Both things seem equally important, equally impossible.

She stops at the edge of the pond and her moving hands are too hard to watch. I bow my head, raise my arms, bend my knees. Water meets over my toes.

The Girl Scouts say that every good Scout should know how to swim. They say it makes other activities possible, for instance, life saving. But they never say whose.

sparks, nv

Most Holy Apostle Saint Jude, faithful servant and friend of Jesus, patron of desperate and difficult cases. The name of the person who betrayed our Lord has caused you to be forgotten, but not by me, and I implore you,

get me the fuck out of here.

(make your request here)

last call

Mama wants her ashes spread on Starvation Ridge, and even the 4-H Club isn't ready to take that trip, but Grandma wants her ashes spread where pretty things grow. She tells me this on my last visit to her, my only visit by myself, a lone Greyhound on a long mountain night, vomiting all the way home. PLEASE, DON'T LEAVE A MESS, the sign in the bus bathroom begs all of us, the drunk and hopeful who make this trip between the trailers in the mountains and the casinos in the desert every payday.

She tells me this before the cancer that she arms daily with generic cigarettes makes its final push. Grandma can hear her death coming, and like Mama, isn't shy to talk about it, but unlike Mama, there's no mystery about how it will arrive.

She's so tiny now, her skin gathers in folds around her shrinking bones like velvet in an old Reno whorehouse. When she lifts her arm, to drop an ice cube into her beer, to light a cigarette butt, I can see both her breasts, her whole torso, through the armhole of her housedress, so shrunk back is she from the size she used to be. Seeing her breasts like that, small like mine but wrinkled and low, they are my future breasts, makes her fragile to me for the first time, and mortal. It is the only thing that makes me understand what I never really did before, that Grandma will soon be no bigger than a blue jay. And as soon as she is, she'll fly away home.

PLEASE, DON'T LEAVE A MESS, the sign repeats, PLEASE, but

maybe that is only my head, only my stomach turning inside out to make this thing an un-thing, a never, the opposite of what I know it is. The truth. The doctors at Plumas County Hospital know she's dying, she knows it too, and as her day draws to an end she holds my hand with sharp, strong fingers and says, "Girlchild, your Mama raised you right and now it's up to you."

I stumble back to my seat, try to time the sway of my heart's sickness to the rolling of the bus on the interstate. The casinos' promises fly by the window on too many billboards to count, their lights reflecting off the top of the suitcase that I'm holding tight to my chest. It's the same suitcase that made the same trip with me when Mama and I were together barely two years before, and the same road rolls beneath us, potholed with words unsaid.

Death is different when it shows up early, invites itself to dinners, and keeps you company for late-night talks about paperwork and affairs and questions about whether a house or a body can ever truly be in order. I keep my suitcase out, ready to go back to visit as soon as more school can be missed without raising the County's eyebrows any higher than I've already done, but before I can use it, Grandma is gone, off to join Mama on the very late shift. I haven't opened that suitcase again, even though I know Grandma wants me to, wants me to fill it up and get myself out.

on the road

Every Girl Scout should know how to follow a map or to make a simple one to direct other people. This, from the Out-of-Doors section of the *Girl Scout Handbook*, under "Mapping." Girl Scouts have long known the value of being able to judge heights, weights, distances, number, and time with reasonable accuracy. I never earned a badge, but I'm no different. I map streets from memory. The streets pulse in a circuit, paved with tar but haloed by streetlamp, the asphalt holy with blood. There is no stain on this road but the accident is always there, happened, happening, about to, we walk around it, watch it ripple in the heat on summer days. Mama is always on her way home here, coming home, home, not home yet. Mama is unscrewing a lightbulb, stumbling, and Grandma writes, forgets, scolds, saves, while the Hardware Man touches, Carol watches, ice cream melts, books are lent, teeth rot, shotguns fire, and the lid of the hope chest cracks open and shut. The streets of the Calle run in circles like the light that shines from Saint Jude's candle, the ring it burns into this table, where I, hands to mouth and hands empty, sit. Some things, having seen them once, you always see.

parcel post

Without Grandma's letters the mailbox is empty forever except for bills, guilty notes from my brothers' wives, the *Penny Saver*, and the final package I don't want to receive, and so I'm avoiding all things postal like a Bible plague, leaving out the back door, slipping silent over the back fence, looking out the back window so I won't catch a glimpse of the mailman and go blind as Lot's wife, salt in the wind. I dream of the back window, of feeding stray pit bulls at night who howl while I push the meat through the torn screen, until noise and the smell of flesh lead the Calle folks to think that I've died too. The Nobility is haunted and they come for my body with Maglites blazing hot as torches on a witch hunt, burning up the front walk until I stumble out the front door and tell the truth about being what I can't deny but hate to admit. Alive. I wake up in a sweat to the sound of the postman's knock and all the back doors and bad dreams in the world haven't made one bit of difference to the blue of his shorts, the heaviness of her remains in my hands, and the fact that I have to sign to receive this package, because when brother Bob drew the short straw and had to go down to Portola to pick Grandma up from her temporary resting place at the Lesley Bros. Crematorium and Funeral Home, he fulfilled her wishes and sent her home to me, right as the mail.

Grandma's box is the same size as Mama's even though she was so much smaller at the end, but the weight is still what's hardest to understand. That, and what I didn't expect, a stack of letters from Mama to Grandma, letters originally sent from the Calle to Cali, now returned to a sender who left no forwarding address. Mama's letters are all bound in string because Grandma saved her ribbon for other things, more permanent, because Grandma knew that soon enough these letters would crumble up and blow away down the Calle like everything else, stick to the fence in some fool's garden, and sprout again with next year's flowers.

a girl scout obeys orders

Ceremonies are ways to mark high occasions in your troop, the *Handbook* tells me, and even though my troop is still a troop of one, I'm marking this occasion high as the watermark that rises and blossoms junk from the landfill. Grandma wanted to be left where pretty things grow, and I'm not sure it qualifies, but I'm taking her to the pond because she did a lot of growing on the Calle, and anything pretty that came from Calle soil is because of her. Mama's ashes will go to the Ridge just like she wanted and Grandma's will stay on the Calle, where I can find her when I need her, feel her between my toes at least, put her grass between my lips. As long as I know where Grandma is, I'll be able to find myself.

One of the smartest things the Girl Scouts say is that sometimes ceremonies that you make up for yourself have even more meaning than the ones you get from books. I guess the weatherman agrees, because as I walk the Calle a warm rain starts and just as it does, the electricity stops. Goes out, quiet, like my bare feet on the night cement. The streetlights disappear in darkness but I can see where they've been, like shadows burnt on paint, marking where portraits of a family once hung. Gravel oblongs in the moonlight where trailers used to be, like so many hands of cards being removed now, their wins and losses banked below them, because every good dealer, god or man, from Boomtown to the MGM

267

Grand, is just another gypsy fortune-teller you pay to make your future known. His hand slides across the darkness now, leaves bills crumpled behind, gathers up the deck, and throws it into the landfill.

savage value

A 1972 Nobility double-wide trailer cost $17,450 when new and will depreciate at a rate of 60 seconds per minute of hurt, shame, and anger calculated at the rate of 4 syllables, or one al-li-ga-tor each. Alligators are savage animals useful for marking off seconds of destruction but unused to being kept indoors. The double-wide has been in use for 16 years and has suffered 5,845 days of depression by hurt, shame, and alligator. If the useful life of a double-wide trailer is 20 years, find the Nobility's salvage value. What is the worth of the trailer after 16 years?

(Show all of your work.)

A) *The alligator will grow to 18 feet in length.*
B) *Together they will make $36 selling scrap metal.*
C) *The woman must exert more than 90 pounds of force to move the stone.*
D) *It will take 2⅓ matchbooks to solve this equation.*

269

fire sale

Old trailers like mine are tinder-boxes, firetraps, accidents waiting to happen, but even so, the Nobility is all I have. I can't sell it, can't bear to think of the examination, the assessment, hopeful hands pulling back the corkboard to check for holes punched in paneling, pulling up Mama's patchwork carpet to look for water damage on the floorboards. That carpet, jumbled and crazy, would be the very first thing to go, as misunderstood as anything good a Hendrix ever made.

According to the Girl Scouts, there are many types of fires, reflective and crisscross, trench and hunter, but they all start with the same basic ingredients, fuel and a spark or two. The stove is surrounded by kindling and I've got plenty of matchbooks. Their covers say THE TRUCK STOP in white letters on a black sky as a semi-truck rolls into the parking lot, its headlights swooping over the bar. Beneath the truck's wheels, smaller letters warn "Close Cover Before Striking" and that's exactly what I do. I close all the covers. The cover of the *Girl Scout Handbook*. The cover of the suitcase over a glass unicorn, river stones, and bundles of letters, the cover of the phone book after looking up the number to the Fire Department and giving them a ring. And then I pick up my suitcase and close the door. Grandma's right. It's time for me to strike out on my own.

A trailer will burn in sixty seconds and I'm going to let it. I'm going to let Saint Jude begin his good work on our homemade curtains, keep his promise to this hopeless cause and make Grandma's God's-Eyes burn bright tonight, burn holes right through the plywood and pressboard of the Nobility's walls and cabinets. I don't own a watch so I keep my own time, count one-alligator as I slip between streetlights and let all the beliefs of the Calle turn into ash, seven-alligator and let the shadows of the Hardware Man turn into smoke, eight-alligator as the smoke gathers and follows my beauty down the Calle to the pond and over those hills to whatever world is waiting for me out there. At twenty-five-alligator a window bursts behind me, and I turn around just in time to see an ember escape the Nobility's core and rise up into the night air, shivering, bright and free.

GIRL SCOUT NOTES AND AUTOGRAPHS

GIRL SCOUT NOTES AND AUTOGRAPHS

YOUR NEW BOOK

This edition of *girlchild* belongs to you.

Official and unofficial Girl Scouts in many different parts of the world have had a hand in this edition of *girlchild*, particularly: Anna Hat Padgett, Lisa McCormick, Paula F.O.S.P. Parnello, Sara Marcus, Sarah Ciston, and Tavia Stewart-Streit. Many Girl Scout leaders, and other adults, also helped to prepare *girlchild*, particularly: Cathy Salser, Judith Remmes, Mamacita Marci Zeimet, Michael Hacker, Thorn Kief Hillsbery, Vicki Forman, and my strong Scouting family. Without the Eagle Scout faith of Bradford Earle, none of this works and the future is a myth. Many thanks, also, to Ben Marcus and Juliette Low for wanting better things for girl-children everywhere.

There are not Girl Scout patches splendiferous enough to award Bill Clegg at William Morris Endeavor for being a true friend and champion, and without the untiring guidance, patience, and grace of Courtney Hodell at Farrar, Straus and Giroux, this girl would be forever spinning her compass in the woods.

I hope you will like this book and that it will help you in your Girl Scouting.

Tupelo Hassman

The U.S. Supreme Court ruling in the case of *Buck v. Bell*
has never been overturned.

discussion questions for girlchild

1. *girlchild* is set in a "town just north of Reno and just south of nowhere." If the story were set elsewhere, how would the challenges Rory Dawn faces change? Or would they? What direct impact does geography have on Rory's life? What about where the story is located in time? Could *girlchild* be set in the 1970s? In the 2010s?

2. *girlchild* is told in short, and sometimes extremely short, chapters. How does this method serve to impact the story? How would it feel to stay with any of these scenes longer than we do? How would that change the overall impact of the novel?

3. There are many stories about Rory Dawn and the Hendrix family that combine in *girlchild*, including the social service report on the Hendrix family, Shirley Rose's hopes for Rory's future, Jo's fears for Rory, the government's position on Rory's culture, and Roscoe Elementary and Junior High schools' opinions of Rory's academic gifts and adventures. Rory Dawn takes each of these for a spin. Why might she do this? What does she gain? Lose?

4. Vivian Buck is, perhaps, Rory Dawn's only friend. Is Vivian real? Historical? Imaginary? All of the above? Do we have any reason to think that Vivian exists for other Calle residents? What does

it say about Rory Dawn if Vivian doesn't exist for others? Does it matter whether Vivian actually exists in real time on the Calle?

5. Dennis is a regular at the Truck Stop and he is one of the few nonvillainous Calle men whose life we see in detail, in the chapter "The Great Strain of Being." What is the importance of Dennis for Rory Dawn? How does he reflect the trajectory of many of the Calle men; for example, Timmy, or Rory's neighbor Marc?

6. Rory Dawn and Timmy have history together on the Calle brought by riding the shifting tide of babysitters. When it is announced that Rory Dawn is advancing to the next level in the spelling bee, she loses her temper with Timmy, throwing his toy truck over the school fence. What other circumstances surround this act of Rory's, and what part of it leads her to turn against Timmy?

7. Jo, Rory Dawn's mother, is a bartender, but this career wasn't always her goal. What do we learn about Jo's early aspirations and why they changed? Does she deserve a second chance? If she were given one, would she take it?

8. Rory Dawn is academically gifted, but instead of this being a boon, it increases her isolation, both from her peers and her mother. Does she find any refuge in this gift? What is the significance of Rory Dawn's throwing the final round of the spelling bee? What does her choice in the misspelling of the word "outlier" (she spells it "outli*ar*") reveal about her feelings with regard to the stratification of her culture? What does it reveal about her place in it?